No Solicitors

John Callas

Copyright © 2017 by John Callas
ISBN: 978-1-7367127-0-2

Published by 14th Street Publishing

First Publishing: November 2017

Cover design by Design Works
Cover design by David Lewis
Editing by: Karl Monger

10 9 8 7 6 5 4 3 2 1

Table of Contents

DEDICATION

This story and film are dedicated to the fans around the world that enjoy the thrill of horror, the discovery of hidden dark secrets, the taste for blood, and a good home cooked meal with a twist of humor.

ACKNOWLEDGMENTS

"No Solicitors," the cult classic film, is represented by VMI Worldwide - Los Angeles, Ca.

CAST

Eric Roberts is an American actor. His career began with <u>King of the Gypsies</u> (1978), earning a Golden Globe nomination for best actor debut. He starred as the protagonist in the 1980 dramatization of <u>Willa Cather's</u> 1905 short story, <u>Paul's Case.</u> He earned both a Golden Globe and Academy Award nomination for his supporting role in <u>Runaway Train</u> (1985). Through the 1990s and 2000s he maintained dramatic film and TV-movie roles while appearing in TV series. His TV work includes three seasons with the sitcom <u>Less than Perfect</u> and a recurring role on the NBC drama <u>Heroes.</u> His sisters Julia Roberts and Lisa Roberts Gillan, and daughter Emma Roberts, are also actors.

<u>http://www.imdb.com/name/nm0000616/?ref_=nv_sr_1</u>

Felissa Rose is perhaps best known for her work in the cult classic Sleepaway Camp franchise, which she began at age 13, playing transsexual murderer Angela Baker in the original film (1983). She is recognized as the number one female villain by Wickedchannel.com. She reprised the role for Return to Sleepaway Camp (2006) and is currently in production on Sleepaway Camp Reunion. She also appeared in Ford Austin's Dahmer vs Gacy (2011), which screened at the 2010 festival. A veteran of more than 50 films, she is a staple in the horror genre both as victim and villain. Rose has also contributed to the acclaimed documentaries Going to Pieces: The Rise and Fall of the Slasher Film (2006), His Name Was Jason (2009), and Something to Scream About (2003). She has been a consultant with festival media partner Fangoria. She travels the country signing autographs for her loyal fans.

http://www.imdb.com/name/nm0741378/?ref_=nv_sr_2

Kim Poirier's been in the entertainment industry for three decades garnering experience as an actor, television host, and producer. She has performed in over 30 commercials and has been featured in countless catalogue and print ads. Some of her television credits include appearing on the Emmy award winning series Mad Men, starring in the Gemini award winning show Paradise Falls, as well as a recurring role on Syfy's Eureka.

On the big screen Kim has had principal roles in Zack Snyder's Dawn of the Dead, Decoys 1 and 2, American Psycho 2 with Mila Kunis, and Silent But Deadly with Jason Mewes to name a few. In addition, a short film she helped produce went to the Cannes Film Festival.

http://www.imdb.com/name/nm0688495/?ref_=fn_al_nm_1

 **Beverly Randolph** is known for The Return of the Living Dead (1985), Return of the Living Dead: The Dead Have Risen (2007) and More Brains! A Return to the Living Dead (2011).

http://www.imdb.com/name/nm0709875/?ref_=nv_sr_1

 **Jason Maxim** is an actor and producer, known for <u>Threshold </u>(2012), <u>Bonnie & Clyde: Justified </u>(2013) and <u>Waiting for Dracula</u> (2012).

Vernon Wells. His first cinema appearance was a minor role in Felicity (1978), a low budget, erotic fantasy film. However, Wells was then fortunate to be cast as the homicidal biker "Wez", in the big budget Mad Max 2: The Road Warrior (1981) filmed in outback New South Wales, Australia. Hollywood beckoned for Vernon, and he spoofed his mad biker role in the popular teen comedy Weird Science (1985), before taking on another villainous role as the treacherous ex-soldier "Bennett", who foolishly double crosses Arnold Schwarzenegger in Commando (1985). Vernon also continued working on television with guest starring roles on The Fall Guy, McGyver, Knightrider, Hunter and TNT.

Vernon has worked on, directed, produced and/or starred in no less than 130 films and countless television shows.

http://www.imdb.com/name/nm0920460/?ref_=nv_sr_1

 **Ken Sagoes** is best known for the role of "Kincaid", one of the Dream Warriors in the classic horror films, A NIGHTMARE ON ELM STREET, 3 & 4, making him the first African-American actor to survive a major horror film and return for a sequel (He also survived in "No Solicitors"). He's also known for John Singleton's "ROSEWOOD" as the loveable "Big Baby" and the role of "Darryl" with Martin Lawrence in the hit series, "What's Happening Now".

http://www.imdb.com/name/nm0756209/?ref_=nv_sr_1

 **Suze Lanier-Bramlett** is known for her work on The Hills Have Eyes (1977), Cut! (2014) and The Hills Have Eyes Part II (1984). She was previously married to Delaney Bramlett. She was the second actress cast as Chrissy Snow for the second pilot of Three's Company (1977).

http://www.imdb.com/name/nm0486839/?ref_=fn_al_nm_1

On this quiet suburban street there's a house like any other . . .

And a family who'd love to have you for dinner.

CHAPTER ONE

Shafts of early morning sunlight penetrate the tall pine trees lining the streets. It is a quiet neighborhood where the wealthy and powerful reside. Children embark on chalk masterpieces drawn on the sidewalk while a jogger paces herself up a gradual incline. Other children play hopscotch and jump rope. A boy rides his bike with a balloon attached to the back wheel, making as much noise as possible, announcing his travels as a car passes. A gentle breeze sends birch leaves swirling downward.

Each house on this street reflects the success of those who live inside. Most are friendly but keep to themselves-- all except for the local busybody gossip hound, Mrs. Rogers, who circulates through the neighborhood cultivating as many rumors as possible. She passes the home of the well-known and respected brain surgeon Lewis Cutterman and his family. The exterior of the house is simple but elegant. There are three large arched windows adjacent to the covered porch. Every window on the main floor is covered in blackout curtains, leaving no possibility for pedestrians to sneak a peek inside. Like many of their neighbors, they do not want to be disturbed by unwanted solicitors. In an attempt to avoid or at least deter them, they have attached a sign over the doorbell. It reads simply: *No Solicitors*.

The interior of the house is warm, friendly, and inviting. The furnishings are both utilitarian and esthetically pleasing, a perfect blend of form and function. A hand-carved fireplace mantle accents the family room, which has a large TV positioned in the corner on a custom-built table.

Lewis Cutterman is a strikingly handsome man. His wife, Rachel, is the head nurse at the hospital where he works, and as such she wields considerable influence over the hospital's decision-making process. They have two children. Their daughter, Nicole, is a beautiful blonde-haired young woman with a wit and charm beyond her years. Their son, Scott, is as handsome as his father and a gifted athlete in all sports, especially his favorite, lacrosse. Both children are excellent students, though neither socializes after school. Instead, they retreat to the security of their home.

To set foot in the Cutterman house is like stepping into a Norman Rockwell painting. They are a loving, happy family who keep to themselves . . . until their peaceful world is disrupted by the ringing of the doorbell by a solicitor who chose to overlook the warning sign.

On the main floor of the house is a locked door leading to the basement. The stairs are made of cement, with an iron guardrail mounted along the open side of the stairs. In the basement is a fully equipped medical facility, an operating room, and a room to process newly arrived patients. In contrast to the main floor, this part of the house, which has been soundproofed and is without windows, has no internet access, and no cell phone reception, is perfectly uninviting. There is only one way out, and that is always kept locked.

Inside the processing room, a terrified young woman in her early 20s is strapped securely to a table, shaking her head back and forth while pleading for her life. Fingers begin to unbutton her dress. She begs her captor to let her go, claiming she will never tell anyone. There is no response. The fingers continue to undo her buttons methodically. She begins to scream and falls into hysterical crying.

"Please, I'll do anything you want. I won't resist you if you want me. PLEASE... Just let me go home to my mom. I don't even know where I am."

After the last button is undone the dress is pulled open, exposing her bare breasts and panties accented with pink hearts. An ominous looking knife is picked up from a nearby table and its blade tested for sharpness. The tip of the knife is placed at her throat then slowly moves down between her breasts, though never penetrating the skin, producing goose bumps that run up and down her entire body. The knife grazes her navel and travels down to her panties. The hand lifts the panties enough for the knife to slip under one side and cut them off. The woman is now fully exposed on the table. A hand reaches over and touches each breast. The right breast is examined and massaged. She pleads. The other breast is also examined and massaged, then it is pulled gently to the side. The woman wails, but to no avail.

The hand lifts one of her breasts and slowly and skillfully begins slicing into it. Her screams tell of excruciating pain and fear. Another hand--someone else's--reaches in with a hot iron and presses it against the now empty blood-soaked breast pocket, searing the skin closed. The woman's pathetic screaming moans are agonizing. Her other breast is pulled to the side and slowly sliced off. The hot iron sears the skin closed as she passes out from the pain.

On the other side of town, in the heart of the city, Lewis is sitting at his desk at the hospital reviewing a file. There is a soft knock on the door, and Sam Nortel, head of hospital administration, enters.

"Hi, Lewis. You got a minute?"

"Sam, with you it is never a minute. But, yes, have a seat. Can I offer you some coffee?"

Sam takes a seat across the desk from him. "No, thanks. Already had too much."

Lewis leans back in his chair. "So what can I do for my favorite head of administration?"

Sam is excited. "I wanted to let you know that you did an amazing job with the surgery on that boy. We all thought he was a lost cause and you somehow managed to pull a miracle. So on that note, I am pleased to bring you some great news."

Lewis tilts his head and has a curious look on his face. "And what might that be?"

"Well, I got a call from the medical board, and they announced that you are being honored as the leading brain surgeon in the country. Congratulations."

Lewis is clearly pleased, his usually stoic features giving way to something else.

"Is that a smile I see? Now that is unusual. Ceremony is in two weeks. Will you be bringing the wife and kids?"

"Thanks, Sam. Let me check with them and get back to you."

Sam leans in close. "This will be really good for the hospital, not to mention the potential financial benefit. Lewis, this is a great honor for you, but I'm still running a business and have a board breathing down my neck about P&L. Well, I'd better get back to work." He stands and shakes Lewis's hand. "Congratulations. This couldn't have happened to a nicer guy."

"Thank you, Sam."

Sam stands up and leaves the office. Lewis smiles and sips his coffee.

"If you only knew."

CHAPTER TWO

Inside the police station, Detective Ralph Swarez sits with a woman who is weeping, clutching a small dog to her chest.

"How long has she been missing?"

Between tears, she stammers, "I think about five days."

"And how old is she?"

"Twenty."

"What was she wearing the last time you saw her?"

"Jeans and her favorite T-shirt, but she loves to wear dresses. She's got a lot of clothes."

"Has she ever disappeared like this before?"

"No, never. Even her best friend doesn't know where she is. I called the school and her work, and they have no idea."

Ralph stops taking notes. "Do you have a recent photograph of her?"

She hands him a picture of her daughter. It is the woman whose breasts were sliced off.

The mother pets the dog.

Ralph calls over a detective to escort the woman to her car. The woman continues.

"I went into her apartment and found the dog was emaciated and thirsty. It doesn't make any sense. She loves her dog."

Ralph looks over at his Chinese American partner, Julie Davenport, who has been listening to their conversation. She knows this is yet another missing person with no leads. Ralph turns his attention back to the woman and hands her his card.

"I want you to take this, and if you hear anything from her please do not hesitate to call me. This officer will show you out now and take you safely to your car. All right?"

She stands and takes his card and they shake hands. In desperation the woman tightens her grip and begins crying again.

"Please find her. She is all that we've got."

"We're going to do everything we can, okay?"

The officer takes her out, and Ralph goes to a cork board and pins the latest victim on it.

"That makes six missing persons in the last three months."

Julie puts down the file she was working on.

"So frustrating. I don't see a pattern or any connection. And we still don't have any bodies."

Ralph looks over his shoulder at her. "Beats the shit out of me, too. Listen Davenport, run a cross-reference on high schools, colleges, clubs, and anything else you can think of. There's got to be some connection."

"I'm on it. I'll also check the hospitals for any John or Jane Does as well as the coroner to see if there are any unidentified bodies."

Ralph turns back to the board. "Come on, people, talk to me. Help me find you."

An ambulance pulls into the emergency area, with interns, nurses, and doctors running to assist the EMTs and police. The entire hospital is alive with activity as a code black has been issued.

A couple is seated in the waiting room. The woman is beside herself with grief. A delivery man wearing sunglasses enters the room and walks over to reception. He is carrying a container marked "Human Organs." As he finishes his delivery, he overhears the man speaking with his wife.

"You know how much Annie loves Maria. She'd give her own kidney if she could. It was a freak accident that both her kidneys got damaged."

His wife is openly distraught. "Accident or not, if she had kept an eye on her none of this would have happened. For God's sake, she is our only child, and if she doesn't get a kidney in two weeks she will die."

He tries to console her. "Sofia, I have been making calls, searching the internet, reaching out to all my business associates throughout Europe. I've even checked all the experimental options. The hospital is doing everything possible. It's not like we can't afford it. And we are close to the top of the waiting list."

"But David, we only have two weeks. I don't care what it takes. You find a kidney for our baby girl."

He puts his arm around her, and as they embrace the delivery man approaches them.

"Excuse me. I don't want to be a bother."

The husband looks up. "What can I do for you?"

"Actually, it's what I can do for you. I have a certain client that gets things for people in need."

The wife pulls away from her husband and studies the delivery man. "The only thing we need is a donor kidney," she says with sincerity.

"Yes, I know."

The delivery man takes their information and tells them he will be back in touch. He explains he has business connections that are available to only a select client list and that it is very expensive. He excuses himself and heads down the street to his car, where he takes out his cell phone and makes a call.

Inside the Cutterman house, Scott answers the phone. On the other end of the line, the delivery man explains what is needed for this couple.

Scott smiles. "Patient's name? Okay, got it. There is a small rush fee so the total comes to $125K. Once we verify the deposit, we will have the kidney delivered."

He hangs up the phone, puts it away, and turns to his sister.

"Well, sis, we have an order for one kidney."

Scott pulls out a small notepad and begins to write.

Nicole is excited. "Male or female?"

"Not that it matters, but it's for a female."

When Nicole tries to look over his shoulder to see what

he wrote he teasingly turns away from her.

"Come on, Scott. How much did we get?"

"$125K."

"Holy shit! You're too much, brother."

"What? It is a rush order. And keep your voice down. You don't want Mom to hear you cursing, do you? You know the punishment for using foul language."

"I'll tell Mom. She is going to be so happy." She calls to her mother. "Mom, I have some good news."

Rachel is in another room. "Oh, okay, I'll be right there."

Nicole turns her attention back to Scott. "She is going to lose her fucking cookies."

Scott leans over to Nicole. "Keep it down or she'll hear you curse. And why is she going to lose her cookies?"

"She has her eye on a new purse, and it costs about $3,000. This way Dad can't freak out."

"Good point. Let's hope the kidney donor and patient are matched for blood type."

"I'm going to call Dad."

Lewis has left the office and is getting into his car in the garage parking area when his phone rings.

"Hello?"

"Hey, Daddy, it's me. We have an order for a kidney." Rachel walks into the room, and as she overhears the good news she high-fives Scott. Nicole continues speaking with her father.

"But I guess you already know that since you have a guy stationed at the hospital looking out for needy patients."

Lewis is pleased. "Okay, one kidney coming up after dinner. Is your mom home?"

"Yeah, hang on. She's right here." She hands the phone to Rachel.

"Hi, honey. How was your day?"

"Well, as my head nurse, you should be the first to know that I am being honored as the country's leading brain surgeon."

Rachel beams with pride. "Lewis, that is so fantastic, and you certainly deserve it. After all, think of all the people you have saved. Congratulations. This calls for a celebration. How about I make your special soufflé for dessert?"

"Sounds great. I have to make a stop on my way home so I will see you in a bit. Oh and, honey, since tomorrow is Saturday and I don't have to be at the hospital, be prepared for some other celebrating as well."

Rachel fans herself. "Exactly what I was thinking."

"See you in a bit." He disconnects the Bluetooth and the radio comes back to life. The song is "Stayin' Alive."

Rachel hangs up the phone and turns to her children. "Okay, kids, let's make this a memorable night for your father. Dad will be home soon, and I want everything to be perfect. In the meantime, would you two please check on our patients' meds and give them their sponge baths and shaves?"

"Okay. Hey, Mom, can I practice my technique?" asks Nicole.

Rachel looks at them dubiously. Scott steps up to his sister's side.

"Come on, Mom. It's not like she can damage any salables since there aren't any left."

Rachel thinks it over. "Well, you have assisted your father and me a lot. I guess that will be all right. You kids go have fun. I'll start dinner." She leaves the room. Scott and Nicole light up at the prospect of playing doctor. They run out of the room, unlock the basement door, and head down the darkened stairs.

Nicole and Scott race down the stairs. The sense of competition between them is friendly but fierce. Nicole falls behind then suddenly pushes an unsuspecting Scott against the wall. With Scott thrown off balance, Nicole is able to gain the lead and beats him into the patient room. The space is dimly lit. There are five hospital beds with three patients hooked up to various pieces of medical equipment. Some are administered morphine to ease the pain and some have tubes protruding out of their bodies and extending over to life support equipment. Even though they are heavily sedated they recognize Scott and Nicole, who are out of breath.

On one side of the room is an oxygen tent. Scott and Nicole walk over to it. Inside is a person whose body is completely splayed open and devoid of organs. The body is being kept alive by machines.

"Scott, unplug everything so we can wheel him into the next room," says an excited Nicole.

Scott enters the tent and begins to pull plugs. Once he

is done, they unlock the wheels. The man's open body twitches uncontrollably as the life support is turned off and he dies.

Looking like a couple of kids on Christmas morning, they roll him into a room made of cinderblock with a cement floor. The place is dismal. All the walls are covered in plastic. The room is equipped with axes, knives, a table saw, a band saw, a sawzall, a drill press, and a wood chipper. They push the gurney over to a long wooden table and maneuver him onto it.

"This is so cool," Scott says with a smirk.

They both put on protective coveralls and a shield for their faces.

"I know, we get to do it all alone now. Finally!" she says as she picks up a scalpel.

Scott jumps in. "Abso-fucking-lutely. And as Dad always says, there is no better way to learn than by doing. Ready, doctor?"

Nicole shows Scott the scalpel. "Ready, doctor."

Nicole skillfully slices the scalp as Scott pulls the skin down over the man's face. Blood oozes from his forehead and trickles down both sides of the face and onto the table, where a pool of blood begins to form.

Scott retrieves a skull-cutting saw. As he turns on the saw and begins to cut the skull open Nicole looks on with delight. When the cut is complete, a portion of skull falls to the floor and rolls around. Nicole looks at Scott.

"Whoops." She reaches down and collects the bone and places it on a table. Scott turns the saw off.

"Okay, Nicole, we are ready to remove the brain." He hands her the scalpel. She steps over to Scott.

"You are one cool brother."

She gives him a kiss on the cheek. She turns to the body and inserts the scalpel between the side of the skull and the brain. She circles the entire brain, skillfully cutting it away from the membrane that attaches it to the skull.

"Okay. It's ready to be removed."

Nicole starts to remove the brain but has to stop because the spinal cord is still attached. Not to be deterred, she gives it a tug. There is a snap, and the brain is free. She gently lifts the brain away from the skull and places it on a tray.

"Good work, Nicole--or should I say 'doctor'? Okay, I'll grind up the bones and mix them with dirt for the garden."

It is now Scott's turn. He takes a saw and, with a few powerful strokes, cuts the head off. Nicole does the same with the hands and feet and places them into a bucket. They roll the body over to a table equipped with a band saw. The blade is turned on. A high-pitched whining sound is heard. This part of the process they are familiar with, and they show no hesitation. Piece by piece they butcher the body with skillful precision.

"Nicole, I'll finish here if you don't mind taking care of our patients like Mom asked."

"My pleasure." She leaves as Scott continues to cut the body into manageable pieces.

Nicole enters the patient room and approaches the frightened victims. William is in his mid-20s and has an athletic build, Priscilla is attractive and in her early 20s, and Jack is in his late 20s and has a small frame. They are all noticeably fearful of her. She approaches them nonchalantly.

"How is everyone feeling today? Now, which of you will it be?"

William musters the strength to speak. "Fuck you."

Nicole spins on her heels and looks sternly at William. "I'm sorry, what did you say?"

"I said fuck you. You and your family are fucking sick."

"Fuck me? Well, that kind of language will cost you." Scott comes into the room and sees the confrontation.

"Is there a problem, Nicole?"

"Well, William here is using foul language, and we all know that is not permitted in our home."

"William, that was not a good thing to do. Nicole, shall we?"

"By all means."

William's arms are tied to the bedrails. The back of the bed is raised to a 45-degree angle. Nicole secures a ring around his head so he can't move. Then she puts a dental gadget into his mouth and opens William's mouth wide. She takes a gauze and wraps it around his tongue. She pulls the tongue out as far as it will go, picks up a scalpel, and slowly begins slicing. William wriggles in pain with each forward and backward motion of the scalpel. Blood flows out of his mouth, with occasional pulses of gushing blood. William's eyes bulge with pain and fear. Every nerve in his body is agonizingly awake. Blood continues to flow heavily as Nicole pulls on the tongue until the last fibers holding it inside of William's mouth SNAP. Once the tongue is completely out, Nicole shoves a hot iron into his mouth to stop the bleeding. He passes out.

"Aww, the poor boy fainted." She looks at Priscilla and Jack. "And if you two even think of telling my mother about me cursing, I'll cut your fucking tongue out just for the fun of it," she warns, holding William's tongue with forceps.

"All set, Sis?"

"Yep. How about you?"

"Yup. The only thing left is to grind the skull."

"Excellent. Nice work, Scott."

"You, too, Nicole. Hey, with all this work I'm getting kinda hungry."

"Yeah, me, too. I'll be up in a minute once I give them their meds."

Ralph and Julie are eating dinner as they work on their missing persons cases. Julie takes a bite of a burger. Ralph is eating junk food. A map is now on the board, with the missing persons photos pinned along the top. Ralph studies the board.

"So the search turned up nothing? Is that what you're telling me, Davenport?"

"Not a damn thing. I have a few calls out to my friends at the bureau. Maybe they will come up with a connection."

"I'm not so sure. This feels local to me. Something about these people just doesn't fit. Did you check with their employers?"

"Yes. They are not connected to any one company."

"Do me a favor. Check with their families and see if any of them know each other. See if they have the same doctor. Get their phone bills, credit card statements - you know, the usual shit."

"Ralph, this isn't my first barbecue."

"Well, somebody out there has a bone to pick."

"Really, Ralph?"

CHAPTER THREE

Coffee is poured, bagels are gobbled, computers are turned on, and the day begins at Sonic Realty, one of the most prestigious firms in town. Their sales force has outsold every other company for the past five years. Leading the company and this morning's discussion is thirty-year-old African American Marvin Grayson.

"All right, people, listen up. Let's all settle down. As you know, we are a no-nonsense group that focuses on results. We don't limit you to any specific territory and encourage door to door solicitation. Please review the packets in front of you. They contain information on how to approach potential clients."

In every real estate office there is an aggressive realtor just like Mindy. In her early 20s, she outfits herself in a style that is both sexy and classy--high-polished nails, lots of cleavage, and not the sharpest tool in the shed. She raises her hand.

"I have a question."

Marvin rolls his eyes. "Yes, Mindy. What can I do for you?"

"Well, just how far can we go to get the listing?"

Marvin has put up with Mindy for the last five years because she finds a way to get listings that yield high results.

"I am not sure where this question is going. Can you be more specific?"

"What I mean is do we bring cookies, or can we flirt?"

"Mindy, I suggest you discover what works best for you as you always seem to manage. If cookies don't do it and flirting gets you in the door, then I don't see any harm in that. But keep in mind you are representing Sonic Realty so be careful not to cross any lines."

Mindy looks at her nails and smiles at the other agents, who do not approve of her approach. They know that given the chance, Mindy would steal every listing they have. The entire office is cautious of her tactics and sneaky ways.

"Well, Marvin, if neither approach works and some of my other ideas don't pan out, then don't be surprised if I never show up for work again."

"We should be so lucky," he says to himself before addressing Mindy.

"Mindy, I know you are resourceful. So go get 'em."

"I have a few ideas that should knock them dead."

Marvin stares at her, bewildered yet again by another perplexing comment from Mindy. "Well, that's all for now. Have a good day, everyone."

Everyone turns back to their folders. Mindy opens hers

and spreads out the map. She positions it different ways. She runs her finger across the surface with her eyes closed. Her finger stops.

"Okay, neighborhood, you're it. Get ready because here I come. I will not take no for an answer so you might as well just invite me in for my pitch."

Mindy's Bluetooth rings in her ear.

"Hello? Hi, honey. How are the honeymoon plans coming along?" She looks at her engagement ring and smiles.

Ralph eyes the cork board with the missing persons photos. Julie walks over. She has been on the phone with her FBI contacts.

"I drew a blank with my guys at the bureau." She looks at the board and wrinkles her brow.

"What's weird is that all of these victims have completely different jobs."

Ralph points at the board. "There's got to be something we're not seeing. These people didn't just vanish."

Julie tries to lighten the mood. "Maybe it was aliens."

Ralph chuckles. "At this point I would take that. Remember the Oberleak case? Not one of the victims was related and they had nothing in common."

"True, but as far as we know we aren't dealing with homicides. We are dealing with missing persons."

"Okay then, what are we missing. Let's start from the top again and see if we overlooked something."

"We have gone over this a thousand times."

Ralph lets out an exhausted breath. "I know. Try going

back into their childhood. See if they went to the same camp or something. *Anything.*"

"You think this might be a revenge situation?"

Ralph leans in close to Julie.

"Honestly, I don't have a fucking clue what's going on here. But with no bodies we have to assume they are together."

"Hey, what if they are all holed up somewhere planning a heist?"

Ralph is clearly frustrated. "Let me get this straight. We have an intern for a political group, a construction salesman, a cosmetics lady, a bible thumper, a census taker, and oh yes, a Girl Scout troop leader selling cookies. My hunch is that they joined forces with the aliens to plan a heist. Yeah, that works."

"Like your ideas are so much better. No wait, you don't have any." Julie walks away muttering to herself in Chinese. Ralph has no clue what she is saying except that it doesn't sound like a compliment.

Having decided on a neighborhood and arriving with cookies, Mindy is prepared for battle—anything it takes to get another listing. She walks up to the house and notices a sign above the doorbell: *No Solicitors.*

"Ha, we'll see about that."

She rings the doorbell, unbuttons the top button on her blouse, then decides to unbutton another one, exposing even more cleavage. She notices her engagement ring and removes it, slipping it into her purse. The door opens. Scott stands there with an open shirt, his remarkable physique on full display. Mindy smiles at the sight of him.

Scott is intrigued by this beautiful woman. "May I help you?"

Mindy gears up and launches into her polished pitch. "Why, yes, I'm sure you can. My name is Mindy, and I represent Sonic Realty. I noticed what a beautiful house you have and was wondering if you would consider selling it?"

Rachel is upstairs. "Who's at the door?"

Scott rolls his eyes. "It's a realtor wondering if we want to sell the house."

"Can you handle it, Scott?"

"Got it, Mom." He turns back to Mindy.

"As I was saying, I have just the client for your house. And by the way, money is no object for this client."

"I appreciate that, but I really don't know how all that stuff works."

Mindy knows the game is afoot. She smiles at him seductively. "I can show you how it all works."

Scott continues to lead the unsuspecting Mindy on.

"So what would be the first step?"

"It would be helpful to see the house."

"When do you want to see it?"

Mindy goes in for the kill. "Well, I have some time now if you are available. How many bedrooms do you have?"

Scott has his own agenda and sees through Mindy's veiled attempt at seduction. He plays along.

"There are four bedrooms. Hey, I have a great idea. My dad is on his way home and since you would have to talk to him about all this anyway, maybe you can stay for dinner."

Mindy senses a major score. "Only if you will be joining us."

"Please come in. I hope you like rump roast."

"Sounds delicious. And I have cookies for dessert."

Scott invites her in. As Mindy enters the house Scott takes a casual glance around the neighborhood. No one is in sight. He closes the door.

Scott stands by the front door buttoning his shirt as Nicole descends the staircase. Mindy's eyes register disappointment as she mistakes her for Scott's girlfriend. Scott picks up on this and relishes the awkward moment. He looks on as both girls shoot daggers at each other. Finally he intervenes and breaks the tension.

"Mindy, this is my sister, Nicole."

Her look of disappointment gives way to a broad smile. She walks over to the stairs and holds out her hand.

"What a pleasure it is to meet you."

Nicole keeps her arms folded and replies frostily, "Nice to meet you, Mindy. Are you here for my brother?"

Scott jumps in. "Actually, Nicole, Mindy is a realtor and is interested in listing our house for sale."

Nicole's demeanor shifts visibly and she breaks out in a smile. "Really?"

"I told her that Dad can go over the details with her. I also invited Mindy to stay for dinner."

Mindy tries to win Nicole over to her side. "I hope I am not intruding on a family gathering."

"Not at all. Why don't we have a glass of wine? Mindy,

do you prefer white or red?"

"Whatever you have open is fine."

"Nicole, why don't you take Mindy into the family room while I get some drinks? We have open bottles of both."

"Okay, then red, please."

Rachel walks over and joins the conversation.

"Mindy, this is our mom," says Scott.

"Nice to meet you. I overheard you will be staying for dinner." She picks up Mindy's arms and examines her unabashedly. Mindy appears put off, but she handles it deftly. "Perfect. Scott, drinks, please."

"Sure, Mom." Scott walks out.

"Tell me, what brought you to our house?" Rachel inquires.

Mindy responds with pride. "Well, to be honest, I just pointed to a neighborhood on the map."

"What about your co-workers?" asks Nicole.

Rachel follows up. "Wouldn't someone already have picked this neighborhood or had it assigned to them by your boss?"

Mindy naively reveals her strategy. "Actually, no. And my boss doesn't have a clue where I am. We get to solicit business wherever we feel comfortable."

Rachel encourages Mindy to disclose more. "I wish I had a boss that didn't care where I was."

Nicole pushes the point to make sure Mindy has told them everything. "Don't you have to call in or anything?"

"No. It is a really cool job. No micromanagement. I am free to do as I choose as long as I get results."

Nicole and Rachel exchange a sly smile. Rachel takes Mindy by one arm and Nicole takes her by the other.

"Well, Mindy, we will do whatever it takes to make you feel comfortable with us," says Rachel with warmth.

"Thanks! You people are *so* nice. I feel like I could stay here forever!"

Rachel nods at Nicole in silent agreement, and they start to laugh. Mindy is clueless as to why they are laughing, but she joins in politely as Nicole and Rachel lead her toward the family room. Once seated, Nicole excuses herself to go help Scott in the kitchen with the drinks and appetizers.

Nicole comes into the kitchen stifling a laugh. Scott is pouring the wine.

"What did you find out?"

"She's perfect. No reporting to a boss and no one knows where she is. Now all we have to do is find out which car she came in and ditch it."

Scott stops pouring. "That will be easy after she's enjoyed the special dinner drink I am preparing for her." Scott shows her the powder. "I'll give you and Mom champagne, and I will have a scotch with Dad, so that we don't get the glasses mixed up."

Rachel and Mindy are chatting away about Mindy's stellar record and about how she doesn't take no for an answer. She assures Rachel that she will get top dollar for their house.

Nicole joins them carrying a tray filled with appetizers. Scott follows with drinks. He sets down the tray and hands them out. Once everyone has their drink, Rachel looks at Scott.

"You are always so good at toasts. How about giving us one?"

"Sure, Mom, love to. Here's to meeting a new friend who we hope will help make us lots of money."

Mindy takes that as a win. "I'll drink to that. Money is a good thing, and I hope me being here brings you lots of it."

Rachel replies, "That's very sweet. I am sure that will be the case."

They clink glasses and sip from their drinks. Mindy shoots a flirtatious smile to Scott, who returns it.

Mindy sniffs the air. "Boy, that dinner smells delicious."

"It is the freshest meat you can get," says Rachel.

Mindy whispers to Scott. "You look pretty edible yourself."

"As do you."

Nicole forces a smile at Mindy before sending a disapproving, jealous gesture toward Scott.

Having run a few errands, Lewis arrives home and pulls into the garage. He thinks about all the people he operated on that day and the lives he managed to save. All the pressure he experienced throughout the day has produced a voracious appetite and a thirst for his favorite drink. Lewis walks up and unlocks the front door and steps inside. Rachel usually comes to greet him, but not tonight. Lewis is perplexed and wonders if the family is out of the house.

"Hello. I'm home."

"We're in the family room," Rachel hollers. "And we have company."

Lewis shakes his head, puts down his things, and joins the others. He kisses Rachel and walks around the couch.

Scott and Mindy stand up.

"Dad, I'd like you to meet Mindy."

Mindy shakes Lewis's hand.

"Nice to meet you, Mindy. Please, have a seat. And what do we owe the pleasure of your visit?"

Scott hands Lewis a glass of scotch.

"Mindy is a realtor. She has clients that might be interested in buying our house."

"That sounds promising."

"We thought we would relax over cocktails and dinner, then show her the house before we move on to dessert," says Scott.

Mindy is quick to add, "And they forgot to mention that I plan on bringing you lots of money."

Lewis smiles. "Well, I'm sure you will. You look very healthy."

Mindy is unsure how to take such a compliment but wears it well, knowing that the house listing depends on her charm and personality.

She looks down at her figure. "I work out three times a week so I am in excellent condition. So tell me, Lewis, what do you do?"

"Actually, I am a brain surgeon."

"Oh. No offense, but the sight of blood makes me

weak."

Rachel smiles. "Most people feel that way. Neurosurgery is very specialized. Nicole, would you help me serve dinner? Scott, why don't you open a nice bottle of wine."

"Please don't go to any trouble on my account."

"Don't be silly, no trouble at all," Nicole comments.

The others leave while Lewis and Mindy finish their cocktails. They clink glasses.

Dinner sits in the middle of the table as the last plate is served by Nicole, who passes behind Mindy and gives her a catty look.

Mindy sniffs the plate before her. "This smells delicious. What kind of meat is it?"

Scott leans in toward Mindy. "See if you can guess."

Nicole glances at them. "Mindy, be careful of Scott. He is a practical joker."

"I grew up with a brother so I am used to that."

She cuts a piece of meat with a sharp knife and brings it to her nose. Mindy slowly puts the meat into her mouth and begins to chew. The family members look at one another and then at Mindy.

"Not sure what kind of meat this is, but it sure is tasty. Scott, maybe I need a little more wine to cleanse my palette."

Scott gets up to pour her another glass. He positions himself so she can't see as he pours something into her wineglass.

As he does that, a bug lands on a Venus fly trap, which quickly closes, capturing the unsuspecting insect. Scott returns to the table with the spiked wine and hands the glass to Mindy.

"Cheers."

Mindy takes a good gulp. Scott sits back down.

Mindy cuts another piece of meat. "Okay. One more bite then I will guess."

She chews it carefully, trying to decipher the taste in her mouth.

Scott continues the conversation. "Glad you are enjoying the meal."

"It's Mom's special recipe," says Nicole proudly.

Lewis adds, "Kind of a family secret."

Mindy stops for a second and ponders things. "I'm going to guess it is a wild animal of some type."

Scott says, "In this case you are close."

"OH, I get it. You hunted this, didn't you, Scott?" She smiles at the idea of the hunt.

"You got me. I made the kill."

"Am I good or what?"

Everyone laughs good-naturedly. She takes one last bite. As she chews some blood trickles downward from the corner of her mouth. She wipes it with her napkin and inadvertently burps.

"My apology. I've never had that happen to me. Must be too much wine."

Rachel looks at her. "No such thing. Wine is the nectar of the gods."

Mindy's eyes flutter a bit.

Scott sees the effects of the drug taking hold and distracts her from noticing too soon. "So Mindy, do you have a boyfriend?"

Playfully, Mindy joins in, slurring her words. "Why, Scotty, are you curious or interested?"

Nicole slides her chair next to Mindy's. "We are all interested."

Mindy laughs. "Family affair? Oh wait, that didn't sound right."

Nicole strokes Mindy's hair, feels her arms as if sizing up a cow, rubs her back, and replies.

"Don't worry, we are a very tight family."

"Nothing kinky, I hope."

"No, of course not," Rachel says.

Lewis explains things to Mindy, sparing nothing. "We are a family business. Rachel is my head nurse, Nicole and Scott run the back office taking orders."

Mindy shakes her head in an attempt to clear it. "I thought you were a brain surgeon?"

"I am, but we have a small side business."

Mindy is trying to focus, but everything is getting blurry.

"What kind of business?"

Scott whispers, "We are in the parts business."

"What kind of parts?"

Nicole leans in close to her ear. "Body parts."

Mindy snaps her head around and is nose to nose with Nicole. "You mean cars?"

Rachel and Scott join Nicole by Mindy's side.

Lewis clarifies. "No, my dear. We work with human body parts."

Mindy is now thoroughly confused. "Wait...wait...wait...When you say human body parts, do you mean you have a tattoo business?"

Rachel picks up Mindy's wineglass. "Here, honey, have another sip. It will help with the transition."

Mindy briefly looks up at a very blurry Rachel. "Transmission?"

She passes out and does a face plant into her meal. Lewis takes his napkin off his lap and walks over to the others.

"Well done. Let's get her downstairs. Just strap her in for now and start an IV so she sleeps through the night. We have a kidney to retrieve."

Lewis lifts her head off the plate to check her pulse. Her face is covered in food. Once Lewis has what he needs he lets go of her head, and her face falls back onto her plate with a thud.

Scott jumps into action. "I'll get her purse and figure out which car she drove here in and get rid of it."

Nicole flutters her eyelashes. "You're so good at making things disappear."

"Why, thanks, Sis."

"You are welcome, Brother. Now help me get her downstairs."

Nicole and Scott strap her to the bedrails, remove her cell phone, and dress her in a patient gown. Nicole takes

Mindy's arm and inserts an IV that is attached to a slow drip of barbiturates to keep her asleep through the night. The other patients look on in horror. Rachel checks Mindy's chart.

"Is everyone comfortable?"

No one responds. They all glance at Mindy, but only for a moment. Rachel goes over to check on William, who is moaning.

"Any pain?"

William murmurs.

Rachel has a soft spot for her patients and doesn't like to see them in pain--as long as they behave.

"Oh, you poor boy."

She goes over to his bed and reviews his chart.

"Well, you are in luck. Nicole, please add a bit more morphine to his drip to ease his discomfort."

"But Mom, he said the 'F' word to me."

Nicole smiles at her mother then looks at William with venom in her eyes.

Rachel ponders what to do. "Now William, that wasn't very nice. Their little brother never understood the importance of not using foul language. May he rest in peace. William, if you promise me not to use that word again I will give you some pain relief."

William is weeping from the pain and fear. He tries to speak but is unable.

Scott watches the exchange between Nicole and Rachel. He sends a sly smirk to Nicole behind Rachel's back.

"But Mom, he can't speak, remember?"

"Well, lucky for him he caught me in a good mood. Give him what he needs."

Nicole walks over to the machine and opens the drip. William's expression registers relief. Nicole would rather see William suffer for challenging her authority, but she doesn't let it show. Lewis comes out of the oxygen tent and joins Rachel.

"Which patient is the kidney coming out of?" asks Lewis.

Scott points to Jack. Lewis nods his head in agreement.

"You check him for a match?"

"Yes, Dad. He is perfect," says Scott.

"Excellent. Let's get him prepped." Rachel and Lewis head to the operating room and prepare for surgery.

Nicole opens the drip and eyes Jack until he passes out, then she and Scott wheel him out of the patient area and into the operating room.

A commercial operating room light is turned on. Lewis takes charge.

"Okay, we need to transfer him to the operating table, then we can turn him over."

They move Jack over and roll him onto his stomach. Rachel preps the surgery site using cleaning solution and sterile padding.

Lewis reviews the medical tools he will use to perform the operation.

"Scott, do you have the donor carrying case ready?"

"All set, Dad."

"Perfect. Rachel, are we ready?"

"Yes, doctor."

Lewis is amused at her comment and plays along using an English accent.

"So formal?"

"After all, I will be assisting the leading brain surgeon in the country."

He continues in his amusing accent. "I suppose you're right, nurse."

She hands Lewis the scalpel, and he makes the initial incision. The four of them work in perfect harmony as they tear away the skin with spreaders to expose the kidney that will be removed. A clock on the wall shows three hours have passed. Lewis looks at Nicole and hands her the scalpel. She becomes visibly excited.

"Here, honey. Time for your first solo. But first tell me: what these are called?"

This is Nicole's big moment. She has been studying medical books for years while assisting her mom and dad during operations. She knows there can be no room for error, and if she is to someday take over as the family surgeon, this is the moment of truth. Scott gives her a reassuring nudge and squeezes her hand.

She takes a deep breath. "They are the right and left renal artery."

Rachel beams with the pride of a mother watching her daughter grow up right before her eyes. Her little girl is taking her first real steps in becoming a doctor.

"Nicole, I am so proud of you. You are going to make

an excellent surgeon."

"My daughter, the doctor," continues Lewis in his English accent.

Lewis and Nicole trade places. She skillfully finishes removing the kidney. Once she has it outside William's body, she examines the organ.

"Judging from the kidneys I've seen, this one looks pretty healthy."

Speaking without an accent, Lewis says, "Excellent eye. This is a good specimen. And good work, sweetheart."

Nicole beams with pride. "Thanks, Daddy."

Scott looks around the operating table. "Hmmm, maybe I should have asked for more money."

"That's my boy."

Nicole places the kidney into the carrying case, and they remove their masks and gloves. Scott closes the case.

"I'll use the disposable phone and call the hospital and tell them the kidney is on the way."

"I'll start him on antibiotics so he doesn't get sick," quips Rachel.

"Thank you, darling. And Nicole, please increase the morphine so he sleeps through the night comfortably."

"Absolutely. Remember the last one that got sick? The meat was not nearly as tender."

CHAPTER FOUR

Ralph and Julie work through the night with what little information they have. They compile photos and other relevant data to try and gain a foothold in their investigation. In the morning, their first task is to check the hospital for any Jane or John Does. They enter the hospital and walk over to the reception station. Nurse Helen runs a tight ship and takes pride in her job. Challenging her authority typically leads to a blunt and straightforward response that most would prefer to avoid. She sees Ralph and Julie approach.

"How may I help you?"

They flash their badges.

Ralph takes the lead.

"This is Detective Davenport and I'm Detective Swarez. We are investigating several missing persons."

Julie takes out some photos. "Do you recognize any of these people?"

Nurse Helen scans the photos. "No, can't say that I do."

Julie asks, "Any Jane or John Does in the ER?"

Nurse Helen finds this question to be insulting. There are protocols that every hospital follows in cooperating with law enforcement.

"No. And as you know, we are required to notify the police if any come in."

Ralph can sense the tension. "Of course. Well, thanks for your help. Here's my card. Please contact me if anything changes."

As they depart the reception station, the delivery man places a carrying case on the nurse's desk.

"Donor organ delivery, order number 3445KDN. Please sign here for proof of delivery."

Nurse Helen's assistant, Mary Jane, signs the paper and takes the case containing the kidney.

"This could not have come at a better time. It's the only thing that can save that girl's life."

She takes the case and walks down the hall to deliver the kidney to the waiting doctors. The delivery man follows her to scope out other potential clients.

Not far away, a doctor is breaking some bad news to a waiting couple. The delivery man is lurking in the shadows and overhears their conversation. The wife is crying as the doctor explains the situation.

"We have done everything we can, but I am afraid your son is in desperate need of a new heart. The valves were damaged beyond repair in the car accident."

The wife is beside herself. "Oh, my God. Please say this isn't happening." Anger builds and she turns to her husband. "Do something. Why can't you do something? You just had to show off again, didn't you? And now because of your macho bullshit I'm going to lose my baby boy."

"What do you want me to say? Tell me, please. I have apologized a million times... I know I was wrong... It hurts me just as much as it hurts you. He's my son, too."

She grabs her purse and slings it over her shoulder. "Just fix it!" Her dramatic departure leaves her husband and the doctor speechless.

The husband goes over to the doctor. "She, umm... She's just... How long can you keep him alive while we wait for a new heart?"

"We have him on life support, but we can't keep him that way for long. Take your wife home and get some rest. I'll prescribe a mild sedative for her and make some calls. Is your cell still the best number to reach you?"

"Yes."

The delivery man walks away from the scene and pulls out a cell phone.

"Hello? I am at the hospital making the delivery, and there is a couple here in need of a heart for their son. They are heading home for a few hours. I'll get their number and pass it along. FYI, some cops were here inquiring about missing persons."

On the other end of the line is Scott, who is in the patient room with his family as they do their rounds. Scott hangs up. Rachel notices Scott's expression.

"Are you okay, dear?"

"Yeah, Mom. Just some cops snooping around the

hospital. Anyway, the good news is it looks like this could be a busy night."

Nicole is reading William's chart and conferring with Rachel.

"What's up, Brother?

"Someone needs a heart. I'll give them a call and negotiate the fee."

"Great! Mom, it looks like you're going to get that new dress."

Lewis looks up from checking William's heart rate. "Dress? What dress?"

"Come on, Daddy. It's such a cute little dress... and it's on sale."

Lewis put the stethoscope around his neck. "Oh, boy. Those dreaded words."

Nicole looks at Scott. "Which words?"

"On sale."

Rachel loves these touching moments of familial fun and bantering. "Now boys, you know how important it is that us girls look and feel great."

Lewis poses the sensible question. "Should I ask how much?"

Rachel smiles. "Not unless you want to be the heart donor."

They all laugh.

CHAPTER FIVE

A small wood chipper spews out white powder as Scott feeds in raw material from a 10-gallon drum. He reaches in and pulls out a skull and femur. He takes the skull and covers it with a towel. He grabs a small sledge hammer and slams it down on the bundle, reducing the skull to small pieces. He throws the leg bone into the chipper followed by the skull fragments. The bones grind into chips and fly into a bin. He is pleased that he will have more food for his rose garden. Nicole joins him. She is admiring an earring. Then she puts it on.

"Are you almost finished? Mom's soufflé is about ready."

"Was it rude that we didn't serve Mindy a dessert?"

Nicole is nonchalant. "Not really. Mom only made enough for four. Besides that, she's trailer trash. Probably doesn't even know what soufflé is."

"Okay... then I guess it worked out perfectly."

Nicole twirls in a circle, showing off her new blouse.

"So, what do you think?"

Scott laughs out loud. "I don't think Mindy will miss it."

Nicole joins in the laughter. "I know, right? Do you need help mixing the chips?"

"No thanks, Sis. I will do that later. I need to call that couple in need of a heart so I can get their permission to get the specs from their doctor to see if we have a match. I won't distribute the chips in the garden until tomorrow."

"Okay, but don't be too long or I'm gonna eat your soufflé."

"Don't you dare," Scott says playfully.

"You've been warned. By the way, Mom needs some milk for coffee in the morning. Want to walk with me to the store after dessert?"

"I'd love to, but I've still got a lot of chipping to do. There were a few extra meals that needed to be processed."

"No worries. Do you need anything?"

"Nope, I'm good."

Nicole squints her eyes and playfully punches Scott in the arm. "All right then."

Scott rubs his arm. "How are we even related?"

She says as she leaves, "Blood, baby. Blood."

The family meal is like something you might find on the table of any typical American family. Cocktails before dinner, followed by appetizers and then the main course. After dessert, Nicole heads to the store to pick up some milk.

Outside the store lurks a stalker. He spots Nicole inside buying milk and quickly realizes she is alone. She pays for the milk and leaves the store.

Outside some skateboarders stop to let Nicole pass. She smiles and thanks them for being gentlemen. From inside a car, the stalker watches as she walks behind the building heading toward the playground. Nicole always cuts through the park because at that time of day it is quiet and the shortest route back home.

Nicole heads through the park and a light flickers then goes out. Thinking little of it, Nicole walks along listening to music. She continues along a pathway now being sprayed by the landscape sprinkler system. Halfway up the path she has a sense she is being followed. She slows down and looks over her shoulder. No one. All is deathly silent. There is no breeze, only the stillness of the approaching evening as the sun sets. She turns back and continues on her way. She crosses over a bridge and goes down another path. She hears a light rustling noise, stops, and looks around. She sees a nearby bush gently moving. A squirrel darts across the path. She is momentarily startled, but this gives way to gentle laughter.

Nicole makes a right turn and continues through the playground, now on the last leg of her trip home. She passes a jungle gym, slide, climbing bars, and swings. Again she senses a presence. She stops and turns around as she pulls her hair back into a ponytail in hopes of glimpsing any sign of danger. After a 360-degree turn she decides all is well.

She continues past the wrought iron gates when, out of nowhere, a hooded figure emerges and grabs her, covering her mouth with his hand.

With Nicole securely in his grasp, he says, "If you make a sound or scream for help, I will snap your neck. I'm going to let go of your mouth. You understand what will happen if you scream?"

Nicole nods her head. He removes his hand and spins her so she is facing him.

"What do you want? Money? I have $50 in my purse."

"I don't want your money. I want you."

He throws her against the wrought iron fence, causing one of her earrings to fall into the bushes.

Nicole tries to calm him down. "Listen. No need to get rough. I love sex... and I've always wanted to do it with a stranger."

She grabs his crotch and starts to rub it. Her assailant grabs her by the hair and forcefully drags her to the ground. He gets down close to her.

"Show me your tits."

"Okay! Okay! First let go of me. You can't be so rough with a lady. Otherwise, you're not gonna get any."

The man looks at her hard nipples. "I want it."

Nicole unbuttons one button and pinches her nipples seductively. "You want more?"

He is now completely distracted as she undoes her blouse one button at a time.

"Yeah. Show me."

Nicole is now fully in control of the situation. After undoing the last button she opens her blouse, exposing her perfectly formed breasts.

The man in the hoodie is excited beyond his wildest

dreams. "Yeah. Yeah, yeah, yeah..."

Nicole gently pushes him back. "Why don't you lie down and let me pleasure you."

He grabs her hand and stops her.

"All right. But one false move and I'll snap your neck like a pretzel."

"I understand."

He lays back and begins to unzip his pants. She stops him.

"Let me do that. It's part of the fun for me."

He agrees and lays down on his back. She unzips his pants and begins to satisfy him orally. He moans as he lets down his guard. While Nicole continues to pleasure him, she slowly reaches into her back pocket, pulls out a switchblade, and flicks it open. She slides it along the ground and with a quick motion slices his dick off in one swipe. He screams in terror and pain. Deftly she maneuvers behind him, grabs his hair, pulls his head backwards, and slashes his throat, the blood muffling his wails of agony. She stands up, with blood trickling from her puffed cheeks and the remains of a penis hanging out of her mouth. She sucks in the last bit like a piece of spaghetti and continues to chew, then finally swallows it. She dabs the corners of her mouth.

"Would've tasted better with mustard."

Ralph is preparing a hot dog with mustard. Julie hangs up the phone and walks over.

"I just got a call that there is a dead body by the convenience store at Forest and Main."

"You got a cause of death?"

"Apparently a slashed throat was the killing blow."

Ralph is about to bite into his hot dog. "What does that mean?"

"Well, it seems he is also missing his penis."

Ralph stops and eyes the hot dog, then tosses it into the garbage can.

He wipes his mouth. "What?"

"His penis is... gone. And according to the uniform at the scene, it was cut off with a knife. And there is no trace of the--"

"Okay, okay," he says, cutting her off, "I get the picture. Sounds like we have a collector on our hands."

Julie looks at Ralph. "Why would anyone want to collect a--"

"I have no idea why any killer collects parts from their victims, but it happens. Let's get there before the scene is compromised."

Julie attempts to lighten the mood. "Good point. We wouldn't want any dick...tective to contaminate the crime scene."

Ralph stares at her, not amused. "Funny, Julie. Very funny. Bring gloves with you."

Ralph grabs his gun and coat.

"Why?"

Ralph puts on his coat. "Oh, I don't know, maybe because you are going to play dick...tective and find me that penis."

"You have no sense of humor."

Ralph is already on his way out. Julie grabs her gun and follows.

"Hey," she calls after him, "at least this isn't a missing person."

With his back to her, he responds, "Gloves... And you owe me a hot dog."

On the way to the crime scene Ralph and Julie go over all the details. The lack of evidence to point them in any specific direction leaves them frustrated. Julie is distraught that her friends at the FBI can find no connection among the victims.

They arrive at the crime scene to find multiple police cars, crime scene tape outlining the area, helicopters flying overhead searching for suspects fleeing on foot, and the coroner's van. Several police officers are searching the area for clues. Ralph and Julie get out of their car and scan the scene.

Ralph walks over to the body, which is covered by a bloody sheet.

"I'll check the body while you search around for clues."

"Got it."

Ralph lifts the sheet and eyes the body. A policeman stands beside him.

"Man, that is some gruesome shit."

The policeman looks at Ralph. "Unfortunately, I've seen worse."

The policeman leaves and Ralph stands up to greet Julie, who holds an earring at the end of a pencil. Ralph speaks with the coroner

"Have you got a time of death?"

"According to body temperature, he's been dead about two hours."

"Thanks, Doc."

Julie tries to lighten the mood. "Good to see you, Doc. How's the family?"

"Doing great, thanks. How's your mom?"

"Really good."

"Okay then, I'll confirm the cause of death ASAP."

As he leaves, Julie shows Ralph the earring.

"Found this by the wall. And incidentally, this kind of jewelry doesn't come cheap. Looks like the perp is a woman."

"Either we have a woman, an angry tranny, or one sick couple working together to do some nasty shit. Bag and tag for forensics."

Mindy comes to and looks around. She finds herself surrounded by other people with tubes coming out of them, connected to various pieces of medical equipment. She panics and struggles to free herself but to no avail. She notices the IV in her arm and starts to scream.

"Hello? Can anyone hear me? Help. Somebody help me, please!"

The bedridden others say nothing. Mindy notices how none of them are struggling to free themselves.

"What the fuck is going on here?"

Priscilla replies, "No one can hear you and there is no escape, so save your strength."

"For what? And what's with the oxygen tent?"

Jack turns his head toward her.

"That's the last stop."

"Before?"

"Before you die."

Mindy starts to panic. "Wait? Did you say die? Why?"

"Did you try to sell them anything?" asks Priscilla.

"Sort of. I am a realtor."

Jack, who has been staring at the oxygen tent, turns his head back to Mindy. "Bad choice of houses. Does anyone know you came to this address?"

It all starts to sink in for Mindy. "No... my boss never asks, and we don't share that information with the other brokers so they can't try and steal the listing."

William shakes his head. "You will never leave here alive."

"I don't understand. Lewis is a doctor and his wife is a nurse. Why would they keep us here and for what purpose? Don't you people have family or friends, anyone who might realize you are missing?"

Priscilla starts to cry. "I'm a single mom. The last time I saw my little boy was when I dropped him off at school. He's only six... Who will take care of him?"

"My mother is in a home and I am all that she has left. It kills me to think of her staring out the window wondering why I never visit anymore." Jack closes his eyes.

William, who is still weak from the removal of his tongue, musters enough strength to explain his situation. "My wife died a few years ago and the kids rarely visit. I have two cats and two dogs. They've been stuck in my apartment since I got here. Must smell great by now. Poor critters."

"I'm confused. What is it that they want from us?"

In a soft voice Priscilla explains. "I'm not sure how to tell you this, but they sell our body parts."

Mindy loses it. "Again with the body parts! What are you talking about?"

"They farm us--for kidneys, lungs, heart, anything they can sell on the black market."

Jack opens his eyes. "And it gets worse."

"How can it be any worse than that?"

"They're cannibals."

CHAPTER SIX

It's the next morning and the neighborhood is waking up, unaware of what has transpired at the Cutterman house. Kids are back on the sidewalk with chalk in hand, bicycles race up and down, joggers appear, and neighbors rush to get to work on time.

Julie is reviewing files as she finishes her breakfast. She has checked and rechecked the information in search of leads—did any of the victims work together, have the same dentist, or have kids in the same class? She grows increasingly frustrated as she comes up empty at every turn, but she remains convinced there must be something that connects them. Why else would they all be missing? She finishes her coffee, pats her dog on the head, and heads to the police station to meet Ralph.

Lewis finishes tying his shoes. Rachel is dressed for work. Scott is waiting to give his father the good news. Nicole joins the others.

"Anyone seen my earring?"

Scott shakes his head. "I swear, Nicole, you are the queen of misplacing things."

"Not everything," she says playfully then punches him in the arm. He looks at her with hands up in surrender. She shakes her head and smiles. Scott hands Lewis some papers.

"Here is our profit report for last month."

"Looks fantastic, Scott."

Lewis stands up and puts his jacket on. "Well, time to get to work. You kids have a great day."

"Thanks, Dad. You, too." Scott smiles, proud to have received a well-deserved "Atta boy" from his dad.

Rachel follows Lewis to the front door then turns to the kids.

"I forgot to take something out for dinner. Nicole, would you please take care of that."

"Sure, Mom. Scott and I were wondering if you would make the appetizers we like."

Rachel looks at Lewis.

"Okay with me."

"Great. Kids, fresh or frozen?

Scott jumps in. "Fresh."

Nicole chimes in. "Agreed."

"Well, that's fine. We will also need a small roast--leave the bone in."

Nicole is eager to start preparing the fresh ingredients for dinner. "No problem. Love you, Mom."

"Love you, too. OH, almost forgot. Please check their charts and see if they need any medication or antibiotics.

We certainly don't want any of them getting sick."

"We'll take care of it."

They all kiss as Lewis and Rachel go out the front door.

The moment the front door closes Nicole and Scott jump into action. "So, Sis, fresh roast and appetizers?"

"Race you."

Nicole takes off, leaving Scott holding the bag. They open the basement door and race down the stairs laughing and into the patient room.

Nicole arrives first. "Beat you."

"Come on, Nicole, you cheated."

"Bullshit. How did I cheat?"

"You pushed me into the wall."

"You're a sore loser."

Mindy watches this exchange and tries to get their attention.

"Excuse me. There must be some mistake. I am not sick so can I please go home?"

Nicole looks over at Mindy then at Scott. "Aww, she wants to go home."

Mindy starts to protest. "My boss knows where I am, and sooner or later he will send the police."

Scott is not amused. "That's not what you told us earlier. And for telling a fib I think you need to be punished. Nicole?"

"Naughty girl. I'll check their charts and adjust their medications. Why don't you take Mindy into the other room?"

The other victims exchange knowing looks. Scott walks

over to Mindy and unlocks the wheels on her bed.

Mindy isn't sure what is going on but knows it can't be good. "Stop. Where are you taking me? This is sick. You can't be serious."

"Wrong. We have a family business to run. Remember? Body parts? And all that hard work gives us an appetite."

"Please," Mindy begs Scott. "I have lots of money. You can have all of it. I will move to another state and never say a word."

As Scott begins to wheel Mindy to the other room, Nicole walks over.

"Then how do you expect us to make a decent living? Do you know how much money has been taken away from private medical practices? It's got to the point that doctors can barely make a profit anymore." She licks her lips. "See you soon."

Scott wheels her away. Nicole grabs William's chart and walks over to his bedside.

"Hello, William. Did you learn your lesson about not talking back to me yet?"

He doesn't respond.

"What? Cat got your tongue? Oops, nope, I almost forgot.... I did. By the way, it was delicious. Now, since you seem to be behaving, I am going to increase your pain medicine so you will be comfortable, okay?"

William turns his head away from Nicole.

Nicole grabs his face and turns it toward her. "I asked you a question, William. You don't want another punishment, do you?"

He knows better and shakes his head.

"That's more like it."

Scott wheels Mindy into the other room. She continues to plead with him, but he pays no attention to her. She looks around the room and sees axes, table saws, drill presses, walls caked in dried blood and entrails, and a floor that is stained dark red. Scott administers her with a tranquilizer and transfers her from the bed to a wooden table. He straps her down securely, making sure her arms and legs are spread wide. She pleads with him groggily.

"Scott, please, you seem like a great guy. I am sure you and I could have a great time together."

Scott reaches over and grabs a vial and a syringe. He slides the needle into the bottle and fills the entire syringe.

"I'm flattered, but no thanks. Now, I am going to give you a few locals of morphine so you won't feel anything."

Scott goes over and strokes her hand. "You have beautiful fingers."

"Scott, please don't do whatever you are thinking about doing."

Ignoring her, Scott lifts up her gown, exposing her panties. He puts a tourniquet on her leg then injects her leg and hand in several places before putting on protective clothing.

"The medicine should take effect immediately. Strong formula."

Mindy is now in tears as she thinks about her fiancée and the possibility of never seeing him again.

"I beg you, please, I will do anything you want."

Scott pokes her leg with a needle to see if the morphine has taken affect. She doesn't react.

Scott leans in close to her face.

"Ready."

"For what?"

Scott bends down and retrieves a sawzall.

She is hysterical. "For God's sake, please, Scott."

"No God here."

He turns on the power tool.

"You're fucking crazy."

As Scott starts to saw her leg off she screams at the top of her lungs. The saw cuts into the flesh as easily as a hot knife into butter. Blood flows as he reaches the bone and cuts through. The sound of the saw going through bone doesn't faze Scott in the least. Finally the leg is off. She tries to struggle, but the loss of blood is taking a toll. Scott takes a finger full of blood from Mindy's leg and tastes it. He grabs a hatchet and turns Mindy's hand over, and with one swift swing the hand comes off.

Mindy passes out.

An egg drops into a bowl, milk is added, and the contents are whipped with a whisk. Bread crumbs are emptied into another bowl. Olive oil is poured into a skillet, and a flame is turned on. Into a large roasting pan is placed part of Mindy's upper leg. Carrots and potatoes are arranged around the roast. A small pan melts butter. The oven is set at 325 degrees. The melted butter is brushed onto the roast, carrots, and potatoes. Seasoning is added. The roast is placed into the oven. Mindy's fingers are positioned side by side on a cutting board. A sharp knife carefully removes her polished fingernails. The rest of the hand is cut into four pieces with a butcher knife. One by one the fingers and four hand parts are dipped into the egg/milk batter then put in the bread crumbs. When they are finished, they are placed into the sizzling skillet.

Scott has been watching his mom prepare the roast. "That looks absolutely delicious."

Rachel dries her hands. "Thank you, dear. Nicole, how are the appetizers coming along?"

Her eyes glued to the pages of a glamour magazine, she points to the stove. "In the pan, Mom."

Lewis has arrived from the hospital and comes into the kitchen.

"Something smells good."

Rachel goes over to Lewis and gives him a welcome home kiss.

"Thank you, sweetheart. Drinks?"

"Sure. Champagne?" asks Lewis.

"With a little crème de cassis, please."

"Scott? Nicole?"

"I'll join, Mom."

"What are you having, Dad?"

"Martini to start, then wine with dinner."

Scott likes the idea. "Works for me."

Scott opens the cupboard and retrieves the shaker and two martini glasses. Lewis opens the champagne, and Nicole checks the appetizers, flipping them in the hot oil.

CHAPTER SEVEN

Julie finishes a call, excitement written all over her face. She gets up from behind her desk and walks over to Ralph, who is staring at the missing persons board.

"I just got off the phone with my friends at the bureau. You know that earring we found?"

Ralph remains focused on the pictures covering the board. "Yeah, what about it?"

"Well, it turns out that only one jeweler in the entire city carries that specific design."

She now has Ralph's attention. "Finally some good news. Let's go tomorrow morning and see what sort of records they keep. Oh, and by the way, the captain wants us to start canvassing door to door to see if we can ID any of these people."

"Okay, I'll get it organized. What have you got?"

He shakes his head. "Not a damn thing. It just doesn't add up. Usually we come up with a body after a while."

"Yeah, fuck me."

"Was that an invitation?"

"Keep dreaming."

"Well, how about--"

"Uh-uh, NO."

Julie studies the pictures and job descriptions.

"That's weird."

"What?"

"Well, each of these people seems to have had a nontraditional job."

"Meaning?"

"Meaning that none of them sat for eight hours a day in an office. They were all out and about."

"Your point?"

"Well, say we are looking for a serial killer. These people would make the perfect victims for him to stalk and attack."

"Assuming you are correct, how does the earring play into that?"

"She could have been an accomplice, someone to lure the victim."

"Then where are the bodies? Hell, at this point I would settle for just a body part."

Scott holds something in his mouth. He reaches into his mouth and slowly pulls it out. What comes out is a finger bone. It is completely stripped of meat.

"Yum. Great seasoning, Nicole. And the meat is so tender it just falls off the bone."

"Thank you, Scotty."

Lewis finishes his and throws the finger bone on a plate with two others like it.

"Agreed."

"Thanks, Daddy."

Rachel is proud that her daughter is as at home in the kitchen as she is in the operating theater.

"I'd like to make a toast."

They all gather close holding their drinks.

Nicole slips next to her mother. "Okay, Mom, you've got our undivided attention."

"First, here's to Dad for his achievement and for being named the country's leading brain surgeon. Second, here's to Scott for his brilliant business acumen. And finally, here's to Nicole for her first successful surgery. I couldn't be prouder of my loving family. To us."

As they clink glasses as the oven timer goes off.

Nicole is excited to sample her seasoning. "Sounds like dinner is ready."

The doorbell rings. They all look at one another.

"More dinner?" Rachel says with humor.

Nicole looks at the family. "I'll get it." She leaves to answer the front door.

Rachel watches her leave then turns to Lewis. "Maybe you should go see if she needs any help."

Nicole opens the front door. Ralph is standing there. Nicole freezes. She begins to say something when Julie steps out from behind Ralph and hands Nicole a package.

"This was on your porch."

Nicole takes the package. "Thank you."

Lewis joins Nicole as the officers present their badges.

"I'm Detective Davenport, and this is my partner,

Detective Swarez."

"Good evening, officers. How may I help you?" says Lewis, assuming control of the conversation.

"May we come in for a few minutes?" asks Julie.

Lewis doesn't hesitate. "By all means, please do."

They step inside. The front door remains open.

"Daddy, I'm going to help Mom with dinner, and I'll put this package in your office." She kisses him and heads off to join the rest of the family.

"Is there a problem?"

Ralph shows Lewis some photos. "We are canvassing the area trying to identify some missing persons."

Julie adds, "Do you recognize any of these people or have you seen them in the neighborhood recently?"

Lewis takes his time looking over the photos. He doesn't want to raise any suspicion by responding too quickly. Julie sniffs the air. Lewis looks up at her. She notices Lewis looking at her and is embarrassed at having been caught.

Lewis answers. "No. Can't say that I have."

"I apologize, but... something smells delicious."

"That's my wife's cooking. Would you like a sandwich to take with you?"

Julie's face turns red. "No thanks, but I appreciate the offer."

Ralph continues. "For our records, can you please confirm that this is the house of Dr. Lewis Cutterman?"

"That's correct, and I am Dr. Cutterman."

"Well, thanks, doctor. We won't keep you from dinner with your family. Here is my card. Please contact me if you happen to see any of these people."

"Thanks for your time. Goodnight."

Lewis closes the door behind them.

Ralph and Julie walk to their car.

"What a nice guy."

"Yeah. It would make our jobs a lot easier if more people were like him."

"I should have taken him up on that sandwich offer. I'm starved."

"Come on. I know a place that serves roast beef sandwiches with a dipping sauce that is to die for. I suggest getting it rare."

"Sounds good to me."

Lewis listens to their conversation to make sure all is good. Once he is convinced, he goes back into the kitchen.

Rachel is showing Nicole the buttons on her sweater. They are made of diamonds. As Lewis enters Rachel hands him back his drink.

"What did they want, honey?"

"All is well. They are canvassing the neighborhood trying to identify some missing persons."

They all exchange a furtive look. After a long, silent pause, they break out laughing.

Scott takes a sip of his martini. "No bodies, no evidence, no crime."

Nicole has always been the practical one and doesn't let anything slip by her.

"Yup. But it is a good reminder for us to vet our potential business prospects. By the way, Scott, are you finished grinding the last of the bones yet?"

"Yep. I will mix and spread them tomorrow."

Rachel changes the subject. "Okay then, that's settled. Dinner is served. Afterwards we have a heart to deliver."

"A 350-thousand-dollar heart."

"Well done, Brother! Mom, looks like diamonds for us."

Rachel looks at Lewis. "Yes, dear, yellow ones... big ones."

Lewis looks at Scott with his palms held up to the sky. Scott and Lewis smile at each other, knowing it is futile to argue when it comes to shoes or jewelry for the girls.

After dinner the family cleans up the dishes and changes into their surgical gowns. Scott is looking over the financials and is elated about this month's run rate. Nicole and Rachel are thinking about jewelry and shoes. Lewis gives some last-minute instructions on what each family member will be responsible for during the pending procedure. Nicole is hoping that she will have an opportunity to prove herself once again, but she also knows that this is a most complex and delicate operation. If she makes even the slightest mistake it could cost the family a boatload of money, let alone her mom and she not getting their just rewards. They all head downstairs to prep William.

In the basement, the family gathers in front of William, whose eyes are open. Lewis steps over to William's side.

"Hello, William. How are you feeling tonight?"

"Honey, he can't talk too well after the naughty word he

used," Rachel says, reminding Lewis of his condition.

Lewis nods his head in acknowledgement. "William, we don't use vulgarity in this house. I hope you have learned your lesson."

Lewis turns to Nicole and Scott.

"Please prep the operating room. And make sure it is spotless."

Scott springs into action. "Got it, Dad."

Nicole wields a syringe. "Should I start William on his pre-op anesthesia?"

Rachel is impressed that Nicole is one step ahead. "Thank you, sweetheart. Yes, please take care of that, and I will get the surgical kit ready for your father."

Rachel and Lewis head to the OR. Nicole goes over to William. You can see in his eyes he would tear her apart if only he could. This does not escape her notice.

"Now, William, you aren't still mad at me, are you? After all, it was you who used that nasty word."

William looks away as Nicole goes over to his IV. "You will feel a slight sensation of cold then you will get tired. Everything will be fine. Daddy is really good at this."

She pushes the needle full of anesthesia into his IV, and soon the pre-op medicine begins to take effect. William's head rolls left then right as his eyes flutter and close for what will be the last time.

"Scott, can you help me roll William over to the operating table?"

"Sure, Sis."

They unlock the wheels and push him toward the

operating room. The other victims watch in horror as they know that what awaits William awaits them all. He will survive the operation but will never wake up or recover. He will be slowly taken apart according to the whims of the family appetite.

William is placed on the operating table and prepped for surgery. IVs and life support equipment are set into motion. Bags of saline and blood are hooked into William's veins. Scott covers the patient's head and places anesthesia tubes into William's nostril and then turns on the gas to ensure William stays out during the night-long operation.

Nicole makes a few final checks. "Dad, William is prepped and ready."

Lewis takes over. "Okay, kids. Ready to proceed?"

Scott makes a few last-minute checks as well. "We're ready, Dad."

Rachel always checks and rechecks to make sure they haven't overlooked anything. "Nicole, please check the patient's vital signs and make sure his anesthesia is balanced."

Nicole knows she did everything correctly but does not dare to challenge her mom. She goes over and checks the machine, making a slight adjustment.

"All set, Mom."

The sheet is removed, exposing William's chest. Rachel hands Lewis a scalpel, and he makes the initial incision. Blood trickles as the scalpel continues down the center of his chest. Rachel and Nicole clean him up as Lewis pulls the skin away to expose the bone he will cut into to get at the heart.

"Saw, please."

Scott picks up the saw. "Here you go, Dad."

"Thank you, my boy."

Lewis saws into Williams's chest to separate the ribs. Bits of bone chip off. Nicole and Scott work to keep the area clear and clean for Lewis and to make sure William does not develop an infection.

Rachel points to a tool. "Nicole, please hand me the spreader."

Nicole hands the instrument to Rachel.

"Ready for the spreader."

Lewis takes the spreader from Rachel and slips it into the cut bone and spreads the ribs apart, exposing the beating heart. He hands the spreader back to Rachel, who hands it to Nicole.

"Scott, you did inform the hospital that the heart was on the way, correct?"

"Yes, Mom. They are on alert."

With the chest spread wide, William's beating heart is plainly visible. "Time to bypass the heart and get him on life support. Nicole, look at this and tell me what you see."

"That is what a 350-thousand-dollar heart looks like," Scott boasts.

Nicole loves a challenge. She has been studying this procedure for years and is ready to put her knowledge on display. "I see the right and left coronary artery, posterior descending artery, left anterior descending artery, and acute marginal artery."

Lewis looks at her with pride. "Excellent. And what is the procedure for transplanting a heart?"

Nicole continues. "You remove the patient's heart except for the back walls of the atria. The backs of the atria on the new heart are opened and the heart is sewn into place. Then you connect the blood vessels, allowing blood to flow through the heart and lungs. As the heart warms up, it begins beating. Before taking the patient off the heart-lung machine you check all the connected blood vessels and heart chambers for leaks."

Scott gives Nicole a hip nudge. "I'm impressed, Sis."

"Why, thank you, Brother."

They all busily work at connecting tubes to William's heart. Once these are secure, Scott turns on the bypass machine and blood flows into the pump that will keep William's blood flowing.

Once Rachel is satisfied that all is working properly, she says, "I think we are ready, Lewis."

"Good work, team. Here we go."

Lewis skillfully lifts out the heart and hands it to Scott, who places it into the travel case.

"Okay, I need to make a call and get this heart to the hospital."

"Be careful."

Rachel wipes her forehead. "Can you stop and pick up some chocolate? I always have a craving after surgery."

"Sure, Mom. Anyone else need anything?"

"I'm good," says Nicole.

Lewis says, "Same here. Thanks for asking."

Scott takes the case and leaves for the hospital.

CHAPTER EIGHT

Scott works contentedly, preparing ingredients for the garden. The roses are the most vibrant and lush in the neighborhood. His well-guarded secret is a mixture of ground up bones and top soil.

On the work table is a large mixing trough. Scott blends the top soil with the powdered bones, stirring the mixture as if he is preparing a cake. As he happily goes about his chore Nicole enters the room.

"Do you need any help?" she says, hoping he will say no. She never likes to get her hands dirty, although she admires Scott's results in the garden.

"Nah, I got it. Well, actually can you hold the bag open while I fill it?"

"Sure."

"That was a cool procedure with William's heart."

Nicole grabs one of the empty top soil bags and holds it open while Scott fills it with his special mix.

"Yeah, no kidding. My favorite part is when you see the

heart beating."

Scott thinks about it for a second. "Mine is the whole idea that you can take a heart out of one person and give it to another person and they can live." Scott starts to laugh.

"Okay, what's so funny, Mr. Giggles?"

"Well, I was just thinking... Wouldn't it be hilarious if one of the clients that we gave a heart to wound up back here?"

Nicole giggles at the prospect. "You mean if we sold the same heart twice?"

They high five each other and continue filling the bags, occasionally giggling.

"I wonder if it would taste the same," asks Scott.

"Like refried beans? Why do they have to refry them anyway?"

"You're not well."

"Look who's talking, Mr. Double Dip."

They finish filling the bags and loosely tie them closed. "Okay, that does it. What do you have planned for today?"

"I thought I would go shopping."

"What for this time?"

"Shoes, silly. What else?"

"I don't know... maybe dinner?"

Scott carries the last of three bags outside. After spreading the first bag around his flower beds he brings another bag over to the next bed, which is close to the sidewalk. Mrs. Rogers, the neighborhood busybody, is walking her poodle, Precious. She stops when she sees Scott.

"Yoo-hoo, Scotty."

Scott has no escape. "Oh, great, here comes Shit-for-brains Rogers."

Mrs. Rogers walks up to Scott. "Well, hello."

"Hello, Mrs. Rogers. How are you today?" he says, struggling to sound polite.

"Just fine, thank you."

Precious goes over to the bag and starts to sniff. Scott looks down and moves the bag away from the dog.

Mrs. Rogers continues. "I just can't believe how beautiful your flowers always look. You must tell me your secret."

Scott moves the bag and the dog follows, straining against the leash. Mrs. Rogers is pulled along. The dog tries to claw at the contents. Scott moves the bag again and pets the dog in an attempt to distract it.

"Now, Precious, you don't want to get that nasty old dirt all over yourself, do you."

The thought repulses Mrs. Rogers as she pulls on the leash. "Precious, come to mommy. I just gave you a bath-- and Scott is right. We don't want dirty feet in our house."

"Listen to your mommy, Precious."

Mrs. Rogers pulls the dog next to her, avoiding its dirty feet.

"Now Scott, I know you are using something special in those beds. If I promise to not tell anyone, will you share your secret with me?"

Scott knows he has to give her something or she will continue to pester him.

"Well, okay, there is a secret ingredient."

"I knew it. I told all the ladies at my bridge club that you must have something special in your garden." She looks him up and down.

"Okay, you win. There are two things. But you have to promise not to tell anyone. Okay?"

"Cross my heart and hope to die."

Scott looks at her, wishing if only that were true. "Well, I use premium grade top soil, throw in some root stimulants, and then I add a small amount of fresh, high quality bone meal."

Mrs. Rogers is absorbing it all. She leans into Scott and whispers in a conspiratorial way.

"Thank you. And don't worry. It will be our little secret."

She takes the dog and walks away as he mumbles to himself.

"If you weren't so old I'd cook you, but you would probably taste terrible. And fortunately for you we don't like the taste of dog meat."

Ralph and Julie drive across town to the jewelry store in search of answers regarding the earring that was discovered at the crime scene. They ring the security buzzer and pass through the first of two doors. Once they are inside the buzzer goes off, allowing them entrance to the store. They walk up to the woman behind the counter. Julie takes the lead.

"Good morning. I'm Detective Davenport, and this is my partner Detective Swarez. We are investigating a lead and would appreciate your cooperation. Do you recognize this earring?"

The woman examines the earring. "Absolutely. One of our finest designs."

Ralph pops the million-dollar question. "By any chance, do you keep records of who purchased them?"

"Yes. There were four sales. Three were by credit card and one was by cash."

Julie looks at Ralph.

Julie asks, "Did the cash customer happen to leave an address?"

"Let me check our records. I'll be right back."

William lies in the death tent with tubes coming out of fresh incisions on his chest. The machines pump blood to keep his vital organs alive. Mindy and the others occasionally glance over at him.

Jack is starring at William. "Poor bastard."

"What do you mean *poor bastard*? We are all headed there," says Priscilla.

Mindy looks at the tent. "Isn't there anything we can do?"

"Not unless you have a cell phone that gets reception down here."

"What about trying to escape?"

Priscilla shakes her head. "Never going to happen. Especially since we're all missing a leg and a hand. And the upstairs door is always locked. No way we will be able to fight off Scott and his sick, twisted sister."

Jack is getting angrier by the minute. "Maybe not, but we might be able to impact how much money they make from selling our parts."

"How do you plan to do that? Eat poison?"

"Nope." Jack starts to get out of bed.

Mindy shakes her head. "Jack, what the fuck do you think you're doing?"

"I'm going to fuck up their profit and loss statement."

Jack holds tightly to his bed as he makes his way toward the tent where William is.

Priscilla is concerned. "Whatever you plan on doing, Jack, they will not take it lightly. And you know what that means."

"Yeah, I know."

Mindy grows concerned. "What *does* it mean?"

"It means they will stop the pain medicine and make it very painful for poor behavior."

"So what are we supposed to do? Just lie here and let them dismantle our bodies, one piece at a time? Listen, my fiancé is very wealthy, and he will not stop until he finds me."

"Honey, I know this isn't easy to hear, but either you die painlessly or you die screaming. Either way you die. I've seen the kind of pain these assholes are willing and capable of inflicting... and you don't want any part of it."

As Jack approaches William he looks at Mindy and then at Priscilla.

"When they discover their assets have been compromised, I will take the blame... and the pain."

Priscilla swells with emotion, knowing what sort of price he will pay for his actions.

"Jack... Why?"

"If I am going to die without ever seeing my mom again, then I want to go out fighting."

Mindy looks at him as if he has lost his mind. "That's not a fair fight. They hold all the cards."

"Not really. I have a little surprise for them."

Jack has reached William.

"William, forgive me for what I am about to do. I know you would want me to do this."

With that, Jack reaches over and turns off the machine that keeps the blood flowing. William's body starts to twitch uncontrollably. Jack proceeds to turn off machines until William's body is calm and the life support machine displays a flat line. Mindy turns away and begins to cry. Priscilla closes her eyes and says a prayer. Jack crosses himself and heads back to his bed.

Scott enters the house wearing his gardening gloves. A buzzer sounds, signaling that a patient is in distress or trying to escape and has become unplugged from the machines.

"Oh, crap. What the fuck is going on down there?" Scott heads toward the basement.

As soon as he enters the basement Scott notices William's machine is off. He goes over and checks his vitals, then he turns to the others, visibly pissed.

"Which one of you dumb motherfuckers did this?"

Jack raises his hand. "I did."

Scott leans over Jack's bed. "What made you decide to

crawl out of your bed and do something so stupid? Haven't I gone out of my way to make you comfortable and pain free? HAVEN'T I?"

Jack stares daggers at Scott. "What's your point? You eat us and farm our body parts!"

"You ungrateful piece of shit. Okay, you want to be a big shot? Let's see how you like it when I take away your pain medication. How does that sound, hero?"

Nicole comes racing into the room.

"I heard the buzzer. What's up?"

Scott points to William. Nicole goes over and checks on him.

"Which one?"

Scott points to Jack. "Jerk-off Jackie."

Nicole gives him a cold look. "Jack, did you get out of bed? I guess we need to make sure that doesn't happen again."

"Good call, Nicole. Please get our play tools while I set up."

"Fuck yeah." Nicole leaves to set things up. Scott walks over to Priscilla and Mindy.

"Normally we would take him into the other room to avoid making you uncomfortable, but in this case it makes sense for you both to watch so you can see what happens when you misbehave. Allow me to introduce you all to the punishment chair."

Jack is slammed into a dental chair, where Scott straps his arms down. Nicole places a block of wood under Jack's right leg. Scott checks the block, making a minor adjustment.

Nicole hands Scott a sledgehammer.

Scott turns to Jack. "By the way, did Nicole mention the movie *Misery*?"

Then like a carnival strong man, he swings the sledgehammer in a wide arc and brings it down as fast and hard as he can onto Jack's knee. Jack's leg bends upwards at a 45-degree angle, causing Jack to scream and Scott to smile.

"Feel that? Well, how about this?"

Scott takes Jack's lower leg and bends it back toward Jack's stomach. Bones snap and ligaments are torn loose as blood spurts from the ruined knee. Finally the back of his knee separates from the leg, the last shreds of flesh giving way. Jack screams again and passes out from the pain.

"Oh, no, you don't. No sleeping while we are having fun. Scott, please give me the medicine."

Scott smiles. "Good idea, Sis. We wouldn't want him to miss out on any of this."

Scott hands Nicole a large syringe filled with adrenaline. She plunges the needle directly into Jack's heart. Jack's eyes pop open and he screams at the pain.

"I think I'll give your leg some pain relief while we work on other parts."

She grabs some small syringes and shoots his leg full of morphine and Jack settles down.

Jack challenges Scott. "Hope you're having fun. Hey, you banging your own sister, Scott? After all, there's no way a sick fucker like you could get a date."

"You just don't know when to keep your mouth shut, do you? All right, big shot, you ever see *Marathon Man*?"

Nicole secures Jack's head so he can't move it and then inserts a dental spreader into Jack's mouth. Scott reaches for a drill gun with a long bit. Once Nicole is finished Scott takes over.

"Ready, Scott."

Scott and Nicole lean over Jack's face on either side of him, a sadistic glow lighting up their faces.

"Now, Jack, this is going to hurt you more than it will hurt me. And for the record, I got laid just the other night."

Scott turns on the drill and slowly drills into one of Jack's bottom molars. The drill screeches as smoke and blood spray out of Jack's mouth. Jack's screams are ear-piercing as the drill bit goes through the bottom of Jack's jaw.

Nicole is laughing. "Oops. You went too far, doctor. Can you fill it?"

"Hmmm. Let me think. A few drops of sulfuric acid might stop the bleeding. Your turn, Sis."

Nicole fills a large dropper from the bottle of sulfuric acid and turns to Jack.

"Jack, darling, this is going to really hurt."

She sticks the dropper into his mouth and squeezes the rubber bulb. The acid smokes and burns through his jaw. Jack passes out again, and they remove the mouth gear.

"Nicole, please wake him so he can see the next step in his punishment. But first give him some morphine in his mouth so all his focus will be on the next procedure."

Nicole numbs up Jack's mouth then stabs another needle into his chest. Jack's eyes bulge open. Blood trickles down his face and onto his chest. The smell of the acid mixes with the scents of burning flesh and blood. Scott takes a scalpel and approaches Jack.

"Having fun yet?" Scott shows him the scalpel. "Did you know that the eyes taste quite good when eaten raw?"

Nicole licks her lips. "It's kind of like sushi with a creamy filling."

Scott teases Jack with the scalpel, jabbing it at him and twisting it in the air. Scott gets closer and closer to Jack's eyes with the scalpel. Jack's breathing becomes rapid.

"Fuck you both."

As Scott takes his eyes off Jack to smile at Nicole, Jack musters enough strength to force his head forward onto the scalpel and deep into his eye socket. Scott jumps back. Nicole looks at him.

"Son of a bitch... He killed himself."

"Isn't that a sin?" says Nicole with a smile.

"I believe it is, but let's not waste a good thing."

Mindy and Priscilla scream at the horror they are witnessing. They call Jack's name while weeping hysterical.

Nicole goes over to Jack and twists the scalpel around the eye, popping it out. She puts it into her mouth and bites down. Some white fluid squirts out. She smiles and wipes her mouth. Scott goes over to Jack and removes the other eye and eats it. Mindy vomits.

Unaware of events transpiring at home, Rachel hands

Lewis some paperwork to sign. The phone rings, and Lewis picks up.

"Hello? Oh, hi, Nicole. What? When? Is your brother there to help you? Oh... got it. We will have to write the rest off as a business loss... Yes, I will tell Mom."

Rachel looks at Lewis as she takes a seat.

Lewis continues on the phone. "No, don't worry, it is fine. Okay, sweetheart, we'll see you later."

"Is everything all right?"

Lewis hangs up the phone. "Yes and no. There was a situation at home, but the kids took care of it."

"What happened?"

"Jack pulled the plug on William and the kids decided to punish Jack."

"Well, that seems fair."

"Yes, but Jack decided to kill himself so we lost two sellable commodities."

Rachel ponders the situation. "Well, not all is lost."

Lewis regards Rachel with inquisitive eyes. "Meaning?"

"We can have liver and onions for dinner!"

Lewis smiles. "You always manage to see the bright side of things. I love you."

"I love you, too. I'll call the kids so they can pick up an onion at the store. We'll need it for dinner."

In her mid-30s and stylishly dressed, Claudette has risen in the ranks of the company faster than any other employee. She has been assigned a staff of six to oversee the launch of a new perfume from France. Jean, who is in his mid-20s, handsome, and fresh off the plane from

Canada, complete with an accent, listens intently to his new boss.

"As I was saying, American men and women have responded very well to our initial launch. However, we want to take a grassroots approach to marketing our product. You all have been selected to target specific areas door to door to test this strategy."

Despite his young age, Jean is an excellent salesman. "How will you divide the territories?"

"Excellent question, Jean. Please see the packages in front of you. They include a map of the area we want you to target."

Francine has been with the company longer than most and was overlooked for the position that Claudette now holds. She is not warm at all to her fellow workers, and she has a reputation for being snooty. She grudgingly opens her package.

"Madame, are we to give away this expensive product to people who may not appreciate the delicacy of fine perfume?"

"Francine, the concept here is to get people talking about it. As the recipients tell their friends about the product and word gets passed around, it will help in our follow-up questionnaire with the people you presented the product to. Any other questions?"

Jean raises his hand. "I know I have not been in this country for very long, but the area you have assigned to me is very low income living. Why waste it there?"

"Jean, every person likes to have bragging rights in this

country. To the less fortunate, having something as exotic as French perfume will give them that right."

"Maybe, but it won't give me good sales."

"That is not the purpose of this campaign. Now, please keep track of the names and addresses of the people you meet and present with our product so we can schedule a follow-up visit."

The staff is dismissed, all of them disgruntled with their task.

Jean sits in his car perusing the map, clearly frustrated with his assignment.

"This is so stupid. Americans will not appreciate French perfume. And to give it away to people in this area is a waste of time. Put perfume on a pig... well, it's still a pig."

He looks at the map again.

"*Bon.* I will not go to this ghetto. Instead I will go to... let's see, no not here... maybe here... Voila! I will show Claudette how to solicit an excellent response. *On y va!*"

And with that in mind, Jean heads toward an unassigned neighborhood to prove he is a consummate salesman who is worth his weight in gold.

CHAPTER NINE

Nicole and Scott are in the cutting room removing internal organs and butchering William into roasts, ribs, appetizers, and ground beef for burgers.

Jack hangs from hooks by his shoulders while Scott slices him open from sternum to stomach as if he were gutting a deer. Internal organs spill onto the floor.

Nicole loves trying to get one up on Scott and decides this is as good a time as any to do just that.

"Okay, Scott, I have a challenge for you... Actually it's more of a contest."

"I'm game. What's up?"

"I'll bet you $25,000 that William's liver will taste better than Jack's."

Scott can see this one coming a mile away. "Really? 25K? Good try, Sis, but that is stacking the deck."

They continue to disembowel Jack and William. Nicole smiles.

"That smile on your face gives you away."

"How so?"

"You know very well that with all the drugs we pumped into Jack in preparation for his surgery his liver will be bitter, even with mom's sautéed onions."

"Okay, you got me."

Scott turns on the sawzall and cuts off legs and arms. Nicole picks them up and takes them to the chop saw, where she chops off hands and feet.

"Nicole, why don't you take the livers up to the refrigerator and I will finish up here."

"You got it."

She grabs the livers and puts them onto a tray.

"Oh and... Nicole?"

"Yes?"

"Don't forget to run to the store for the onions."

She smiles at him. "Sure thing... And who knows? Maybe I'll grab an appetizer while I'm out."

Later that night Nicole sits watching a zombie film on TV. Scott comes in, his hair wet from his shower.

"How can you watch that crap?"

"I find it entertaining."

"That shit gives me nightmares."

"That's because you're afraid of your own shadow. Remember when we were kids and you--"

"Will you ever stop bringing that up?"

"I just find it hysterical that I scared you so bad you peed your pants."

Rachel and Lewis join them. Lewis glances at the TV.

"What's this one called, Nicole?"

"*Zombies from Galaxy Effo.*"

Rachel looks at the TV then at Scott. "I am surprised Scott is watching."

"I'm not. I just finished my shower. How was work?"

"Same stuff, different day."

Lewis looks over at her and smiles.

She returns the smile. "Well, it was."

"Kids, I have a surprise for you."

Nicole loves surprises. "Do tell!"

"Your cousin has arranged to have some time off and will be coming over for dinner this week."

"When?" asks Scott.

"We're not sure which night. It depends on which shift he has to work."

The doorbell rings. Nicole is excited. "Mom, Dad, is tonight the night?"

Rachel looks toward the front door. "No. I wish it was. Nicole, will you go see who is at the door?"

Nicole gets up and runs to the door, still convinced it is her cousin. Rachel and Lewis look at each other than at Scott.

"It really isn't your cousin."

Nicole opens the front door with a huge smile.

"Hello, Cuz..."

Standing there is Jean, who is all smiles.

"*Bonsoir.* My name is Jean."

Although she is disappointed, Nicole is nonetheless happy to see a handsome man standing there.

"Well, hello to you. Is that a French accent I detect?"

"*Oui.* I am French Canadian."

"How may I help you?"

"If you have a few minutes, it would be my pleasure to introduce you to some fine perfumes from France... at no cost to you."

"Perfume? Well, what woman wouldn't want to try perfume... especially for free? Please come in and meet the family."

"I hope I am not interrupting anything?"

"Not at all. We were just going to have cocktails before we started dinner."

"Well, if you are sure."

"Of course. Don't be silly. Come in."

Jean enters, and Nicole closes the door behind him.

"Did I mention I love French cuisine?"

After Nicole has introduced Jean to the family, Rachel asks her children to prepare some appetizers for their guest.

Nicole and Scott head to the kitchen to ready drinks, cheese, and bread. Nicole can barely contain her excitement.

"How cool is that? Another one has wandered off the path and into our humble home, said the spider to the fly."

Scott smiles at her joke. "I love European cuisine. I guess it's because they grew up on food that wasn't so heavy into pesticides."

"Tell me about it. That shit can kill you."

"All right, Nicole, I got the cheese and bread. You bring the drinks... and remember which one is Jean's."

"You see the little rings at the bottom of the stem?

Those tell everyone whose glass is theirs."

"You are one smart biatchi."

"Why, sir, you flatter me."

"Shall we?"

They pick up the trays and return to the family room.

Scott and Nicole carry the appetizers into the family room and set the trays down on the coffee table.

Jean cannot believe the incredible generosity displayed by this family. "*Mon Dieu. Quelle belle. Le fromage, du pain, et le verre de vin rouge. Un Français de rêve...* Oh, pardon my manners. I said My God, how lovely. Cheese, bread, and a glass of red wine. This is a Frenchman's dream."

"I hope you like the wine."

"You are too kind. And I hope you like the perfume. Would you like to try some now?"

Rachel agrees. "Yes. But first let's have a toast. To our new friend Jean. Welcome to our home. We hope you stay a while."

"Thank you. I could stay here forever, with your kindness."

Lewis lifts his glass. "I'll drink to that."

Nicole catches Jean's eye and winks at him. He smiles slightly and nods. Then he takes a healthy sip of wine.

"*Bon!* The wine is excellent."

Nicole eggs him on. "Another toast. To the French and their wonderful culture."

"You flatter me." Down goes another sip.

"Jean, do you have a wife or girlfriend?"

Rachel jumps in. "Nicole! That is terribly rude."

Scott smiles.

Jean comes to her defense. "Please. It is fine. I was sitting here wondering the same about Nicole."

She holds up her hand and shows him there is no ring there.

"Completely single."

"*Moi aussi* - I mean, me also." He turns to Rachel.

"With your permission, perhaps you will consider allowing me to take your daughter out for dinner one night?"

Scott nearly coughs up his drink. "Not unless she has you for dinner first."

Everyone laughs except for Jean.

"I am sorry, I don't understand. Have I been indiscrete?"

"Not at all. Its just American women are more aggressive than French women."

"I am not so sure about that, *mon ami.* But I take it that it is okay then?"

"By all means," says Rachel.

Now Jean is in the mood. "May I propose a toast?"

Lewis lifts his glass. "Please do."

"I toast that we all become very good friends, and you like the perfume samples," he says, adding as he looks at Nicole, "and we get to have dinner together soon."

They all raise their glasses. Jean finishes his wine. Scott takes Jean's glass to the kitchen for a refill. Jean takes out perfume samples and passes them around to the girls. He also hands one to Lewis.

"Lewis, this perfume is very special for men. I prefer this over most. It is delicate yet alluring to the women. Try a little on your arm to see how it is on your skin. As you know, everybody's skin reacts differently to perfume. I am sure your wife will like it and perhaps it... well... it... will set the mood?"

Jean is starting to sway a bit. "Pardon me. I must have drank too much wine. I am feeling a bit tipsy. Is that the correct word?"

Rachel calls to Scott. "You can hold off on the wine now. I think he's had enough."

Nicole goes over to Jean and sits next to him. She puts her arm around him and leans his head on her breast.

"Actually, Jean, it isn't called tipsy. In English, it's called drugged."

Jean passes out, and the family routinely goes about getting him to the basement to prepare him.

Ralph and Julie are sitting across from each other at their desks.
Julie slams a file closed.

"It's been days, and all we have is a few people in different parts of the city saying they saw these people."

Ralph looks up from the case files he has been sorting through.

"Yeah, and with that, the captain feels the canvassing was a bust and so we've been reassigned."

Julie looks at him. "Wait... wait... wait... What about the missing cases we were working on?"

Ralph holds up a newspaper with a girl's picture on the

front page. The headline reads: *Mayor's Niece Kidnapped – City-Wide Search.*

"*Were* working on is correct. The entire city has been assigned to the kidnapping of the mayor's niece. So our missing persons are going to cold storage."

Julie's blood pressure increases with every passing second. "So we just walk away? What about the fucking earring? That is a solid lead!"

Ralph goes over and sits on her desk.

"Jules, I know you are dedicated to your work, but sometimes we have to walk away. The resources just aren't there for us to chase ghosts."

"Ghosts?"

"Look, without any leads or a shred of evidence, the captain will catch hell from the city attorney for spending resources that might show we aren't working in the best interest of the public."

She is now fully pissed. "So the public will feel safe seeing every law enforcement officer focused on the kidnapping because we don't have anything to parade in front of the cameras?"

"That's just how it works."

"It's bullshit."

CHAPTER TEN

The following morning all is quiet in the neighborhood. It is a clear, warm day. Lewis and Rachel are awake and lying in bed. Lewis is reading *Secrets*, and Rachel enjoys a cup of tea.

"Good book?"

"Excellent. Can't stop reading. Suspense, espionage, conspiracy theory - what's not to like? Do you have a busy day today?"

"The usual. How about you?"

"Seeing a few new patients who will more than likely need surgery."

"The kids seem so happy these days."

"Can you blame them? Business is up and our Swiss accounts are bulging."

"Lewis, I'd like to suggest we change things up."

"What do you mean?"

"I mean with the house. You know how I love to move into a new house every so often so I can redecorate it.

Change is good."

"You certainly do get restless."

"Restless? We've been five years in this house."

"Okay. We can start to look around if that will make you happy."

"Oh, Lewis, I love you. You are the best husband a woman could have."

She kisses him.

"I love you, too."

"I'll tell the kids they can cut two roasts from Jean and freeze them. We have enough leftovers for a few days."

"What about appetizers?"

A hand-operated meat grinder is locked onto a table. Sitting alongside is a tray holding two severed breasts. Scott gingerly picks one up. Blood drips from the hanging pieces of flesh left over from the amputation. Scott lowers the first breast into the grinder and cranks the handle. The ground meat that comes out will be prepared with flour, butter, and some olive oil for appetizers later that evening.

Jean's leg is cut off in the same manner as Mindy's leg. Then a hatchet severs Jean's hand, and he screams wildly. His leg is taken over to the band saw, where Scott skillfully cuts it into two roasts.

"Nicole, would you please wheel Jean back to the patient room and start the antibiotics... and some stronger pain meds?"

"Sure thing."

She looks at Jean, who appears utterly terrified.

"What are you doing?" he pleads. "Why? Please, Nicole,

we can still be together. I will not tell anyone about this."

"Now, Jean. How could I possibly date a man with one leg and one hand? That would mean I have to do all the chores by myself. Does that sound fair to you?"

"You Americans are fucking crazy. People know where I am. You will be arrested."

"Now now. Lying isn't going to help. You told us how you came to us... Oh and we have a house rule. Any vulgarity will be harshly punished. Just ask your fellow patients."

"You mean there are others here?"

"Of course, silly. How else do you expect us to eat?"

"Eat? Eat what?"

"You, of course."

She wheels him out. "Ladies, I'd like you to meet Jean. He is French."

Later that day during the family rounds, Lewis and Rachel stand at the foot of Jean's bed. Jean is asleep.

"Oh good, Gene is resting," Rachel says in a motherly tone.

Nicole looks over at her mother. "I gave him a large dose of morphine to get him through the night... and Mom, it is pronounced Jean, not Gene."

"That was very thoughtful of you, dear, and I am glad those French lessons paid off... but we're in America. His name is Gene."

Nicole is speechless. Lewis and Rachel walk over to Mindy and Priscilla.

"Hello, ladies. Let's have a look at your charts."

She begins with Priscilla.

"You seem to be doing fine." She moves on to Mindy and studies her chart. "And I'm happy to report the same for you. Any pain?"

"Rachel... Please let us go. You guys must have more than enough money to disappear and never be seen again. For the love of God, please let us live."

This draws Lewis's attention. "I agree that we have enough money, but we like living here in the states. Going on the lam would mean giving up my practice, and if that happened a lot of people could die, without my surgical skills to save them--or worse, they could be left invalids."

Priscilla is incensed. "You can't be serious. You farm people for parts and then eat us. And now you talk about saving lives?"

"It's apples and oranges."

Rachel adds, "We don't kill people for the sake of killing. We need nourishment just like you, except we don't go to the grocery store, where everything has been processed and neatly packaged."

Mindy is shaking her head. "What the hell does that mean?"

Nicole brushes Jean's hair, fluffs his pillow, and straightens out his bed sheet.

"It means that we hunt and live off the land. We prepare our food naturally. We don't buy packaged meats."

She walks over to the end of Jean's bed. "You 'civilized' people seem to think that since you didn't see the animal slaughtered it is okay. Well, we do our own work here, and we don't waste any parts like slaughterhouses do."

"I don't believe what I am hearing. You actually think this is acceptable?"

Scott comes into the room and joins the discussion.

"A lot of tribes use all parts of the animals they hunt and kill, so there is no waste. We do the same, but we are also saving lives by selling your parts."

Priscilla is beside herself with anger. "What about us?"

Nicole counters, "Are you serious? It was you, every last one of you, who came to this house with your own personal agenda. You think you can intrude on people's privacy any time you feel like it without any consequence?"

Lewis adds his own two cents. "You all saw the sign: *No Solicitors,* but chose to ignore the warning. What part of *No Solicitors* didn't you understand? So don't blame us for your Death By Solicitation. The only ones at fault here are you."

Scott drives the point home. "And if you think about it, you are just one person. With your body parts we can save many lives. So your life in exchange for several seems reasonable to us. Plus we get to eat well in the process."

Mindy has come to the end of her reasoning. "You all are murderers, no matter how you justify it. Why don't you just kill us and let us be in peace?"

Scott looks up from his tablet. "Because your organs would spoil faster than we could sell them."

Rachel sees that the patients are getting riled up. "Lewis, kids, I think we are upsetting them. Kids, please top off their meds and meet Dad and me upstairs for cocktails."

Rachel and Lewis leave the room. Nicole and Scott go

over and make some adjustments to the drips. Rapidly Mindy and Priscilla fall asleep.

Scott touches Mindy's foot. "Night, Mindy."

Nicole responds sarcastically, "Aww, Isn't that sweet. Why don't you join Mom and Dad upstairs and I will finish up here."

"Cool. See you upstairs."

Nicole looks over at Jean. He is sound asleep. She smiles, goes over to him and strokes his hair, and leans close to his ear. She takes his ear lobe into her mouth and softly sucks on it, then gently squeezes it between her teeth. A single drop of blood trickles. She tears off a small piece of his ear, chews it, and swallows.

"Ooh, *quel gout delicieux tu vas avoir, mon ange cheri. Dors bien.*"

She licks his cheek.

"Sorry... I mean, Ooh, you are going to taste so delicious, my sweet angel. Sleep well."

The house is lit by the light of a full moon. All is quiet. The family is fast asleep. Each room houses a secret that will lie dormant for another day.

The stillness of the night is shattered by the sound of breaking glass in the back of the house. A black gloved hand reaches in and unlocks the door. A female burglar enters quietly, pans the flashlight around the darkened room, and listens for signs that anyone is stirring. Once convinced all is well, she starts scanning the area for valuables. She cautiously makes her way along the hall, occasionally glancing behind her.

As she reaches an opening in the hall, the burglar enters the kitchen, where she opens drawers and empties them of silverware, putting it into her bag. She moves around the kitchen looking through other drawers when she notices a purse on the countertop.

"Oh, hello. What do we have here?"

She opens the purse and looks inside. She pulls out a wad of crisp $100 bills.

"Yeah, baby. That's what I'm talking about."

She continues looking through the purse and discovers an iPhone.

"Cool."

She searches some more, stops suddenly, and removes her hand slowly. In her fingers she holds a diamond-studded tennis bracelet.

"Diamonds! A girl's best friend. This house is a goldmine! Let's see what else this place has to offer."

She is about to leave the kitchen when she sees the refrigerator and stops.

"I could use a bite to eat."

She opens the door and notices some sliced meat under saran wrap. She pulls it out of the refrigerator, gingerly closes the door, and places the sliced meat on the counter. She unwraps the meat, picks up a piece, and holds it at eye level. Then she sniffs it.

"Smells all right. Probably some exotic meat for the rich folks."

She puts it in her mouth and chews, then promptly spits it out.

"Man, whatever it is that shit's nasty. Fucking rich white people. Why can't they just have some bologna?"

She leaves the rest of the meat on the counter and peeks around the darkened corner of the kitchen to make sure no one is awake. She walks through the hallway looking around. She sees a small desk and opens it, discovering a Monte Blanc pen.

"Excellent. Something to write home to mother with."

As she smiles at her own joke she notices a door next to a painting of a clown. She makes a face at the clown and returns her attention to the door. She jiggles the knob but it is locked.

"What do we have here? Wonder what is behind door number one."

She takes out a pick and jimmies the lock open.

"Piece of cake."

She opens the door slowly and steps inside. With a swipe of her flashlight she illuminates stairs leading down into the darkness. The steps are made of concrete so she is not concerned about squeaky floorboards. She cautiously descends the stairs, guided by her flashlight. Upon reaching the bottom she walks into the patient room.

She pans the wall with her flashlight and locates a switch. She flicks it on and sees Mindy, Priscilla, and Jean. She drops her flashlight.

"What the fuck?"

Mindy wakes up.

"Don't be scared. We are being held prisoner. Can you please help us get out of here?"

She walks over to them and sees the tubes and bandaged hands. She is noticeably repulsed.

"Damn, bitch. What's up with this shit?"

"We don't have time to explain, but the short version is they are selling our body parts."

Priscilla wakes up.

"Who are you?"

"I'm Santa Claus. I don't know what's going on here, but all I want is to rob these people."

"Well, these people are animals. They are taking our parts and eating us as well."

"Say what?"

Mindy explains, "They are cannibals."

"You fucking with me?"

"No, I swear to God."

The burglar looks up toward the kitchen.

"Then the meat I put in my mouth was..."

Priscilla completes her sentence for her. "Probably one of us."

"Man, that is some fucked up shit."

Jean stirs and moans. The burglar looks over at him.

"I want ice cream. The candle has fire. Yes, mommy, I want to go swimming. *Je ne veux pas aller à l'école.*" He falls back asleep.

"What the hell was that about and what's with the tubes?"

"They are feed tubes and for pain medication. Listen, I will explain it all later to you and the police," Mindy pleads.

"Look, lady, I'm a burglar. I can't get involved in this

shit, and in your condition you will only slow me down."

Mindy tries again. "You can't just leave us here."

"Tell you what. When I get to a public phone I'll call the cops. They can sort all this out."

Priscilla's eyes widen. "Behind you!"

The burglar turns around and sees Nicole, who is holding a large syringe. Nicole lunges forward. The burglar grabs Nicole's arms and they wrestle. The needle gets close to the burglar's neck but is pushed away before it can penetrate the skin. The struggle continues as the burglar tries desperately to avoid the syringe. Finally she manages to knee Nicole in the groin, knocking her to the floor, and she runs out of the room. Nicole shakes her head and stands up. She sees Mindy and Priscilla staring at her.

"What the fuck are you all looking at?"

Mrs. Rogers is walking her dog past the Cutterman house when she sees the burglar sneaking out of the house and making a run for it. She takes out her cell phone.

"That looks very suspicious. Let's see... Local Police is speed dial #3."

Ralph is at his desk looking over some papers. The phone rings.

"Swarez."

On the other end of the line a voice says, "Hello, I want to report a burglar in my neighborhood."

"And where exactly is that?"

"Well, I am at Dr. Cutterman's house on Valley Road. I saw a stranger running from the side of his house."

"Your name, please?"

She is incensed that her voice isn't recognized. "This is Mrs. Rogers."

Ralph drops his pencil and leans back in his chair.

"Ah, yes, Mrs. Rogers." He yawns. "Well, thank you for calling it in. We will send somebody to check it out."

Mrs. Rogers continues to talk as Ralph hangs up the phone. Julie looks over at him.

"I take it that was the neighborhood nut case?"

"One and the same. No need to send anyone."

"What a piece of work. Doesn't she realize we don't have the resources to chase her ghosts?"

Ralph shakes his head at Julie's comment.

CHAPTER ELEVEN

The family is gathered for breakfast before Lewis and Rachel head off to work.

Tension fills the room. If the burglar comes forward the family might be exposed. Nicole's failure to secure the burglar has shaken her to the core. Lewis tries to lighten the mood.

"I spoke with your cousin this morning, and he will join us for dinner tonight."

Nicole is having a hard time concentrating. "Oh... cool. Mom, is everything going to be all right?"

"Well, Nicole, I really hope so. Don't feel badly, honey, we'll figure it out. Scott, you know how your cousin loves our ribs with BBQ sauce. Can you cut up some for dinner?"

"Sure, Mom, there's plenty in the freezer."

"Perfect. Please do it soon so the meat defrosts and gets to room temperature. Meat always..."

Nicole jumps in. "Cooks better when it is at room temperature."

"Well done, young lady. You'll make a good cook one day. Oh, Scott, would you please check on our French delicacy and make sure he is properly tied and medicated?"

They all share a laugh. Then they all kiss and say goodbye. Lewis and Rachel leave. Scott turns to Nicole.

"I'll go down to the freezer and get the ribs ready."

"I'll check on the liquor and make sure we have enough single malt and wine for Cuz."

"Perfect - off we go."

Nicole makes a sweeping gesture indicating that he go first. "After you."

She laughs and takes off. Scott smiles and shakes his head.

On the way to the meat locker, Scott stops to check on the patients. He turns on the daytime lights, which are brighter than those used in the evening.

"Morning, campers. Everyone sleep well?"

Jean is groggy but awake. "I don't understand how you can do this terrible things."

Scott checks Jean's drips and makes an adjustment.

"*These... these* terrible things." Scott shakes his head. "French delicacy, my ass."

Scott goes over to Mindy and Priscilla and checks their drips.

"Well, everyone seems good to go. I have some work to do."

Scott completes his rounds and walks across the cutting room to a large metal door. He puts on a coat, hat, and gloves before entering.

"Don't want to get sick."

Scott pulls the door open and enters. The door closes behind him, leaving him in the dark. He finds the light switch and flips it on.

"That's better."

Hanging from meat hooks are various parts of legs and arms. Scott passes by shelves labeled "Roasts" that contain several freezer bags. On another shelf are hands and feet. Toward the back of the freezer are torsos on meat hooks. Scott spins a few around, examining them.

"Ah, these two look great."

He lifts a torso off the hook and sets it down. He does the same for another one. He grabs a torso in each hand and heads back out the door.

Scott goes over and places the frozen torsos on top of a table. He removes his weather gear and slips into his butcher uniform and goggles. He turns on the band saw and cuts the first torso in half. He trims off the remains of the breast bone and then cuts the ribs into appropriate sizes.

"This is going to be a feast for a king."

After basting the ribs with barbecue sauce Nicole puts them into the oven and closes the oven door. She turns and smiles, pleased with her accomplishment.

"How's that, Mom?"

"Excellent. I am very proud of you. A toast to our family's new cook."

They clink glasses.

"Let's hope you have Mom's flare for seasoning."

Lewis comes to Nicole's defense. "I have faith in her,

Scott. I was watching, and she used the same seasonings as Mom so I suspect they will turn out mouthwatering and delicious."

Nicole goes to Lewis and kisses him on the cheeks.

"Thanks, Daddy."

She goes over to Scott and punches him on the arm playfully.

"What was that for?"

"For not supporting me. Hear me roar, dude."

The whole family laughs. The doorbell rings. Nicole and Scott smile.

"Now who could that be?" Scott says with a smirk.

"Our Cuz, you dork."

"Duh! Geez, maybe the seasoning has affected your sense of humor."

"Shall we get the door?"

"After you, Lioness."

Nicole takes a step forward. Scott pushes her away and takes off.

"Oh, you're just lucky I'm wearing heels."

They head to front door. Lewis and Rachel smile lovingly at their children.

"Dr. Cutterman, we have great kids."

"Yes, we do. No other kids like them."

Scott and Nicole open the door to find Ralph standing there. They don't say a word. They are expecting Detective Davenport to peek around from behind Ralph. They continue to stare at Ralph. He enters the house and closes the door behind him. Scott and Nicole are frozen in place.

Ralph reaches into his jacket pocket and pulls out an evidence bag, which he raises to eye level.

"You lose this?"

There is an uncomfortable silence as Nicole and Scott stare at the earring. Then Nicole smiles.

"Cuz. You found my earring!" Scott hugs him, and Nicole gives him a kiss on the cheek.

Ralph looks hard at Nicole.

"Lucky for you all attention is on the kidnapping of the mayor's niece so it wasn't hard for me to take this out of the evidence locker without being noticed."

He hands her the earring.

"Sorry, Cuz."

"All right, so how are my favorite relatives doing? And what smells so good?"

Nicole proudly announces, "I made dinner."

Scott replies, "Still want to stay?"

Ralph laughs.

"Yep. What is it?"

"As if you didn't know. Ribs!"

"Yum, my favorite! How about a drink?"

Rachel is standing at the oven basting the ribs as Scott assists. Nicole pours a scotch for Ralph. She walks over and hands him the drink.

"Thanks, Nicole."

"You're welcome, Cuz."

Lewis and Ralph break away from the family and have a chat.

"So about the burglar. Will you be able to find out if

there is any need for concern?"

"I'll get some fingerprints while I'm here and take them down to the station tomorrow and run them. That should tell us whether she operated alone or is part of a crew."

"Thanks, Ralph. You're a good man."

The oven buzzer goes off.

Ralph gulps his drink. "That sounds like dinner."

CHAPTER TWELVE

Ralph calls Lewis on his personal cell phone so as not to raise any suspicion amongst the other detectives, especially Julie. He looks at a file containing a photo of the burglar and her rap sheet. Lewis picks up.

"Hi Lewis, it's Ralph."

"What did you find out?"

Ralph turns around to make sure no one is listening. Julie is across the room filing forms on another case. She glances over and sees Ralph on his cell but is out of earshot.

"All is well. She's a small-time junkie, nobody with a long rap sheet. Mostly first and second story jobs. This kind of scumbag never comes forward. And if she does, it will land on my desk. In that event we can make sure she disappears for good."

"That's a relief."

"Hey, please thank Rachel for dinner last night. Very tasty. Nicole has a good feel for spices, just like her mother."

"They will both be happy to hear you enjoyed the food.

How is the search going for the mayor's niece?"

Ralph lowers his voice more. "We have a suspect in custody, and it looks like we got our man. Oh... I completely forgot to tell you last night that the captain had us put the missing persons into our cold case files. So that should end that little problem."

Julie heads over toward Ralph's desk. As she approaches Ralph closes the file.

"Listen, I gotta run. We'll talk later, okay? Ciao."

Julie stands in front of Ralph's desk. She glances at the closed file but thinks nothing of it.

"How was dinner?"

"Really good."

"What did they cook?"

Ralph leans back in his chair and puts his hands on his chest. "Ribs."

"You are one lucky bastard to be surrounded by such loving family members. Especially ones that know how to cook. You have to have me over for dinner one night."

Ralph smiles at her.

"I'll see what I can arrange."

The family is gathered for a meeting.

Rachel is smiling like someone bearing good news.

"Kids, your father and I have an announcement to make."

Nicole looks at her. "Don't tell us you are pregnant?"

Lewis shakes his head in disbelief. "Where did that come from?"

"Well, you are adults and you do adult things."

Scott is sitting next to Nicole on the arm of the couch. He pats her on the head.

"Nicole, you have issues. So what's the news?"

Rachel continues. "Your father and I have decided it is time to move."

Scott and Nicole look at each other. Nicole raises her hand.

"I call dibs on first choice of rooms."

Scott objects. "No way. You got it last time."

"Oh yeah, that's right. But if there is a bedroom with its own bathroom I am sure you will be a good brother and let me have it."

"Now something like that will require some careful negotiating."

"I know what that means. I'll be doing your chores for... ever!"

Scott leans down next to her. "And then some."

Lewis smiles at the exchange. "So in preparation, Scott, you will need to sterilize the cutting room and the freezer. We have to make absolutely sure no traces can be detected."

"Got it covered, Dad."

Rachel chimes in. "Nicole and I will call my brother's moving company to take care of the heavy lifting. We will wrap all the equipment so it isn't noticeable by any snooping neighbors."

"What about the salables?" asks Nicole.

"We will not take in any more business and wait until we deplete the inventory. After we have relocated we can start up again," explains Lewis.

"And I was just starting to like Jean."

"Maybe you and Mom can make a French sauce with dinner."

Nicole lights up. "Mom?"

"Sure, honey."

Moving day comes, and the family watches as the last of the boxes are taken to the truck. They all stand in the entrance to say goodbye to their house. They recall all the delicious meals, the family gatherings, and the fun times in the basement.

Lewis looks around. "This house has been great to us. We all should thank it and wish it well with the new owners."

"Of course, dear, but a change is always good," Rachel reminds Lewis.

Nicole waves at the house. "Bye, house. I'll miss all the great meals we had."

Scott is already embracing the practical side of the move. "I am glad the new place has room for a larger freezer."

"Speaking of the new house, can we discuss that bedroom, Scott?"

Scott smiles wickedly. "Of course, Sis. I have a few thoughts on the subject."

Nicole knows what that means but doesn't mind since she knows her brother is a loving person and always attentive to her every need.

CHAPTER THIRTEEN

Scott is outside the new house placing the **No Solicitors** sign over the doorbell. He surveys the new neighborhood with fresh eyes.

"Back in business."

Nicole comes up from behind him and puts her arm around his shoulder. She looks around and smiles. Then she whispers in his ear.

"Lunch is served."

A cloth roll is untied and opened. In each slot is a different knife, each more ominous than the next. A female hand touches each one and then makes a selection. It is a ten-inch-long serrated blade.

Posted on the wall over a bed is a newspaper clipping showing a photo of the mayor's niece and the headline: "Citywide Search Expands for Mayor's Niece".

Tied to the bed below the clipping is a young woman. She is hysterical.

"WHAT DO YOU WANT? My uncle is the mayor, and he

can make sure you get anything you ask for."

The female figure is now standing at the foot of the bed. She raises the knife close to the young woman's face. Panic sets in again.

"You'll be found out. YOU'RE FUCKING CRAZY."

Standing there holding the knife is Ralph, beautifully dressed in full drag. He smiles and takes a step toward her.

"You, my dear, are going to taste delicious."

The young woman lets out a bloodcurdling scream.

Blood sprays on the newspaper clipping and all goes quiet.

The End

EPILOGUE

The Cutterman's have moved to their new home and are happily settled. Their stock is low so they hope you will come visit and stay for drinks and dinner.

They promise to make you comfortable and an internal part of the family.

BEHIND THE SCENES

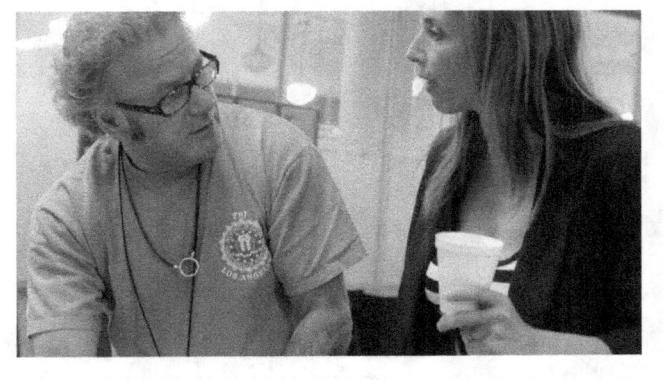

Director John Callas with Producer Felissa Rose

Eric Roberts with John Callas

Prepping for the next scene.

Eric reads "Secrets"

Eric Roberts and Beverly Randolph rehearsing.

Family rehearsing scene.

Eric and John discuss scene.

John and Felissa have a laugh with Robbie Patton with
cue card.

Eric and Beverly rehearsing.

John reviews blocking with Kim Poirier.

Kim and Jason rehearse scene.

Family rehearsing scene.

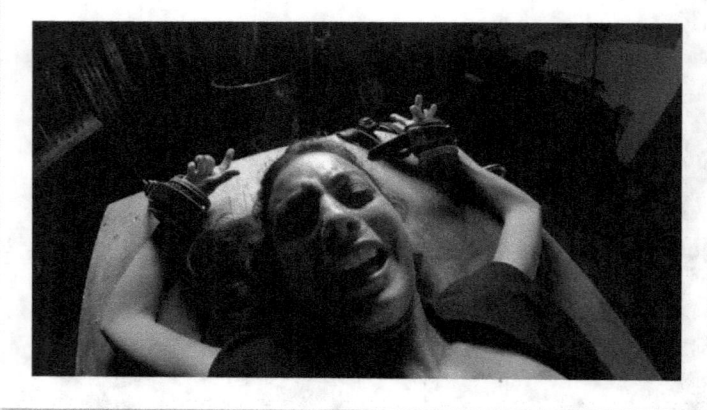

Victim about to die.

Detective Davenport (Serein Wu) tells Detective Swarez
(Joshua Benton) that the victim is missing his penis.

Jason Maxim (Scott) prepares dinner.

Eric Roberts takes a quiet moment

D.P. Howard Wexler prepares a shot.

Crew

Lucy Walsh as Mindy.

The family having fun with a boney appetizer.

Vernon Wells shares a moment with John Callas

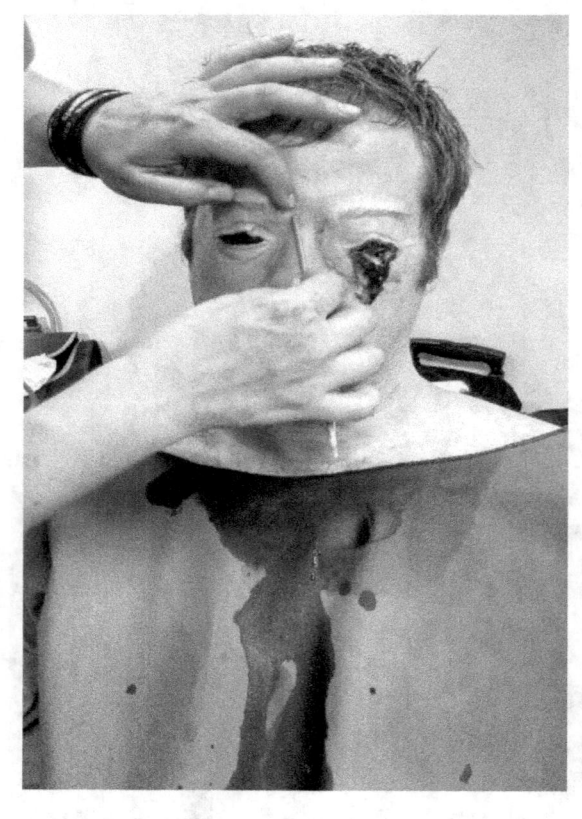

Special Effects being applied.

Lucy having fun with the director.

Scene leading up to removing his tongue.

Ken Segoes as Marvin

ABOUT THE AUTHOR

John Callas is a veteran writer /director /producer in the entertainment business. His experience ranges from the worldwide release of feature films to numerous motion picture trailers, national and international commercials, live action title sequences, laser disc projects, a documentary shot on location in Russia, as well as having been the Worldwide VP for The Walt Disney Company while working at a large post production facility. John recently wrote and directed the feature film "No Solicitors" starring Eric Roberts and is currently adapting NY Times bestselling author, William H LaBarge's book, "Lightning Strikes Twice."

John's prowess can be seen on live action teasers for Ransom, Dennis The Menace, Body Of Evidence, The Golden Child, Spaceballs, The Glass Menagerie, Cocoon II, Poltergeist III, Betrayed, My Girl, Glenngarry Glenn Ross, As Well As Title Sequences For The Two Jakes and A Few Good Men and a promotional film for an amusement ride from Showscan. John also directed an award-winning short film THE WHITE GORILLA.

While creating live action teasers for feature films, John had the opportunity to work with notable actors including Mel Gibson, Walter Matthau, Jack Nicholson, Madonna, Eddie Murphy and Mel Brooks.

In addition to working on feature film teasers, his work can be seen in projects for HBO, The Disney Channel, Show Time, the Broadway Play Phantom Of The Opera and the 1993 redesigned TRISTAR LOGO.

John's extensive background also includes over 200 commercials for such clients as Kellogg's, Dodge, Sunkist, Sprite, Toyota, Fuji, Volkswagen, Honda, McDonalds, Mazda, Minolta, Jedi Merchandising, Kraft, Jordache, Sea World, Givenchy and Sonassage with celebrity George Burns and industrial projects for Corporations including Vidal Sassoon, Salomon North America, Nissan and The Kao Corporation Of Japan.

John's television experience includes directing a 14-week series entitled Potentials, with guests Buckminster Fuller, Norman Cousins, Ray Bradbury, Gene Roddenberry, Timothy Leary and others. He also directed 80 segments for Bobby's World, which has been rated the #1 show on Fox

11 Television in its time slot; garnering John an Emmy nomination.

A multi-faceted filmmaker, John's work can be seen in music videos for Glenn Frey Of The Eagles, Bill Wyman Of The Rolling Stones, Jefferson Starship, Sammy Hagar, Rick Springfield, Doobie Brothers, Styx and more.

For his work John has been recognized with: An EMMY nomination for *Bobby's World*, THE NEW YORK CRITICS CHOICE AWARD for *Lone Wolf*, several awards for his short *THE WHITE GORILLA*, A CLIO and BELDING for his work on the *Sunkist* campaign, the prestigious BEST OF THE WEST for his directorial work on a one-woman show, and an MTV AWARD FOR BEST CONCEPT for Glen Frey's *Smuggler's Blues*.

John holds a Master Degree from Occidental College, and is a member of The Directors Guild of America. He lives in Santa Monica with his wife, Linda and has two sons, Stephan and Nicholas.

www.ingramcontent.com/pod-product-compliance
Lightning Source LLC
Chambersburg PA
CBHW071259130626
46556CB00003B/1378